IN LOVE WITH MY CUDDY BUDDY 2

WRITTEN BY:
MZ. BIGGS
&
TYANNA

Synopsis

Pow... That was the only sound that could be heard resonating through Mace's strip club when Taylor finally walked in and caught her husband, Sincere in an awkward position with Devyn.

Learning that Sincere had a secret life outside of their marriage was enough for Taylor to be ready to sign those papers. Running right back to Chaz, will Taylor really be ready to let Chaz love her the way she deserves?

Chaz, being the knight and shining armor that he's known to be, is ready and willing to accept Taylor when she comes running back to him. While he's prepared to love Taylor unconditionally, he makes it known that he will not deal with her going back and forth between her husband and him. Will Chaz be able to deal with all the baggage that comes along with having Taylor in his life?

When the smoke has cleared and Sincere's life has flashed before his eyes, he's determined to step up and be the man that Taylor wanted and needed him to be, but is it too late? With all of his dirty laundry being aired out, he doesn't know which way to turn. One thing he does know, is that he is not willing to let Taylor go without a fight.

Devyn's reluctance to get over on any and everybody ends up biting her in the end. As a result of trying to blackmail Sincere, she ends up biting off more than she could chew when her scheme backfires on her and causes her to almost lose her life. Is she ready to let go of her conniving ways and be the mother and woman she was destined to be?

Will Sincere be on the winning team? Will Taylor realize what's best for her and open herself up completely to loving another man? Will Chaz get the love he's always wanted? Will Devyn prove her naysayers wrong by turning her life around for the better?

Take a ride with us and watch how everything plays out in the finale of In Love With My Cuddy Buddy....

Acknowledgments for Mz. Biggs:

As always, an Honor is given to God for allowing me to continue with this journey as an author. There have been so many obstacles placed in my path that has given me numerous thoughts about giving up, but GOD is all I can say. Without him, there is no way that this would be possible.

Shan, thank you for allowing me to always think outside the box and try to be different. The fact that you are open minded and allow your authors to take risks is wonderful. I've seen a tremendous growth in myself as an author since I've been published under you. I'm so glad to be a part of the Shan Presents family.

Twyla T., you've become more than my pen sister. I look forward to the daily laughs that we share. I can't even get on the phone now without my children hollering out "Hey Twyla" and half the time it's not even you. I think it's funny because they don't like a lot of people, but they love you. I am grateful to you for always lending me an ear to vent, your endless support, and your honest feedback.

Renisha "Queen Ree" Coleman, I swear to God you keep me laughing. I love that about you. I appreciate the fact that you will read my books and give me honest feedback no matter if you think I'll like it or not. That says a lot about you as a person. Most people feed off the fact that people will tell them what they want to hear, but I can assure you that your honesty helps me to grow in my craft. Thanks for being so real and never changing who you were to appease anybody. Also, a BIG THANK YOU for helping Tyanna and I come up with our title.

Tyanna, my bookie, working with you has been great. Who would've known that working on a collaboration with someone you've never spoken to before, would lead to such an amazing bond? I tend to reach out to you a lot when I'm frustrated now, that's because I keep my circle small. You should feel special being included in it… Lol, I'm kidding, but I do want to tell you that I am glad that we met and that we can lean on each other no matter what's going on.

Big shout out to Tay Mitch for allowing us to utilize him on both of our covers for this series. He's what we based our character, Chaz, off of. Follow him on Instagram at taymitch_. Let me not forget to mention that if you're looking for a healthier lifestyle, he's your go-to guy. Check his "This Really Werks" products out at www.thisreallywerks.com. Thanks again Tay.

Readers, I couldn't forget you. Your support is the reason any of us are able to continue to write. As always, I'm asking that you leave your honest feedback on either Amazon or Goodreads. You can also reach out to me personally. Enjoy ☺

-Mz. Biggs

Check Out My Other Great Books:

See What Had Happened Was: A Contemporary Love Story (1-3)

My First Taste of A Bad Boy (1-3)

Dirty South: A Dope Boy Love Story

Falling for A Dope Boy (1-2)

Feenin' For That Thug Lovin (1-3)

Jaxson and Giah: An Undeniable Love (1-2)

Finding My Rib: A Complicated Love Story

Want to connect with me? Here's how:

email: authoress.mz.biggs@gmail.com

Twitter: @mz_biggz

Instagram: mz.biggs

Goodreads: Mz. Biggs

Facebook: https://www.facebook.com/authoress.biggs

Author Page: https://www.facebook.com/MzBiggs3/

Look for my Reading Group on Facebook: Mz. Biggs Reading Group

Acknowledgments for Tyanna:

I will start off by thanking God for giving me this gift to write. I also would love to thank my lovely readers. Without you guys, I wouldn't have made it this far. My family and friends that have been rocking with me since day one, I love you all, and thanks so much. Author Mz. Biggs, thank you so much for letting me work with you on my very first collaboration. I had so much fun working with you, and I hope we can do it again real soon.

Finally, I can't forget about my Shan Presents family, my publisher, Shan, for giving me a chance, and my pen sisters for all the support. Thanks again to everyone that has ever rocked my cover, shared my link, recommended my books, one clicked, read, and reviewed. You all are very appreciated. I hope you all enjoy this banger, and please be sure to leave a review.......

Author Tyanna's Catalog

Down to Ride for A King

Down to Ride for A King 2

Down to Ride for A King 3

He's Young But He Loves Me Better

He's Young But He Loves Me Better 2

Upgraded by A Street King

In Love with My Cuddy Buddy (collaboration with Mz. Biggs)

Falling for An Outlaw (collaboration with Tina Marie)

Contact info:

Facebook: Tyanna Coston

Instagram: @author_tyanna2016

Contact me via email

35tyanna.coston@gmail.com

<u>Chapter Guide:</u>
Where We Left Off: *Taylor*

Chapter One: *Taylor*
Chapter Two: *Sincere*
Chapter Three: *Devyn*
Chapter Four: *Chaz*
Chapter Five: *Raven*
Chapter Six: *Keon*
Chapter Seven: *Taylor*
Chapter Eight: *Sincere*
Chapter Nine: *Devin*
Chapter Ten: *Chaz*
Chapter Eleven: *Raven*
Chapter Twelve: *Taylor*
Chapter Thirteen: *Sincere*
Chapter Fourteen: *Devyn*
Chapter Fifteen: *Chaz*
Chapter Sixteen: *Keon*
Chapter Seventeen: *Raven*
Chapter Eighteen: *Taylor*
Chapter Nineteen: *Sincere*
Chapter Twenty: *Devyn*
Chapter Twenty-One: *Chaz*
Chapter Twenty-Two: *Taylor*
Chapter Twenty-Three: *Sincere*
Chapter Twenty-Four: *Devyn*
Chapter Twenty-Five: *Chaz*
Chapter Twenty-Six: *Taylor*
Chapter Twenty-Seven: *Sincere*
Chapter Twenty-Eight: *Nyla*

Where We Left Off…
Taylor

Sincere hadn't been gone a good seven or eight minutes before I hopped up to get dressed. We were supposed to spend the day together, but instead of going to the spa and all that other shit he said we would do, the only thing we did was sit in the house. I was in the room watching television, and he was in his office doing God knows what. When he got ready to leave, he called himself coming to give me a kiss, but I curved his ass. I had to pretend to be the same angry woman I usually was when he would leave me. That was the only way I could keep him from being suspicious.

For some reason, I felt relaxed. In the back of my mind, I knew I was finally about to get the push I needed to leave Sincere's ass for good. Although I'd never caught him cheating, something in the back of my mind told me he was up to no good. All of those so-called, late night meetings, trips out of town on short notice and canceled plans couldn't solely be because he had to work. I needed to see for myself what was up. I desired to see who the other woman could be if it was another woman. Sometimes, that nigga was so concerned with his appearance I thought he might have been a little on the sweet-tart side.

Just the thought of Sincere cheating on me had me borderline mad. Sneaking up on him may not be the best idea, but it was better to find out if he was being truthful now than to wait for something to pop up later. I didn't want to spend another minute in an un-meaningful marriage.

"Baby, where are you?"

What the fuck? I thought as I realized that Sincere had come back into the house. Hearing his footsteps coming up the stairs, I jetted back over to the bed and made sure to pull the covers on top of me.

"Baby?" He peeked his head through the doorway.

"Yes. Everything okay?"   I asked like I really gave a damn.

"What you doing back here? You're going to be late for your meeting, aren't you?"

By the time, I'd finished my question, my cell phone rang. I ignored it and peeked over at Sincere to see what he was doing. Instead of him telling me why he was back at home, he stared at me with a coldness in his eyes.

"So, you gonna sit there and act like your phone not ringing?"

"It ain't nobody but Raven. She don't want shit. I'm trying to figure out what made you come back home. You changed your mind about going?"

"Of course not. I left my cell phone under the sink in the bathroom."

"Under the sink? What the hell would your cell phone be doing in there?" My phone rang again and Sincere never took his eyes off me.

Determined to find out who was on my phone, Sincere walked over to the bed and removed it from under my pillow. I was thankful it really was Raven. Chaz texted me earlier, so I briefly thought it would be him. That was the real reason I didn't budge when I heard the phone ring.

"What Raven?" Sincere yelled.

He put it on speakerphone, so I could hear.

"Nigga, ain't nobody call your punk ass. Where my girl at?"

"My wife is in bed minding her business like your ratchet ass should be. I don't know why she chooses to hang with a hood rat like you."

He was wrong for disrespecting my girl, so I had to speak up.

"You tried it, nigga. Don't ever talk to my girl like that again. She's been there for me more than your ass has ever been."

"I know that's right. Tell his muthafuckin' ass, sis. That shrimp dick ass nigga talking all that shit when he acts more of a pussy than us. Fuck outta hea' with that."

And that's why Raven was my nigga. She wasn't having no bullshit when it came to me.

"Raven, shut your dumb ass up." He threw the phone at me, then tried to walk out the door.

"Raven, lemme' call you back."

I ended the call, then jumped out of bed.

"Why the hell did you need to put your phone under the sink?"

I marched up behind Sincere trying to figure out what he had to hide.

"Because I didn't want the steam and shit to get inside of it while I was in the shower. Gone back and talk to that bitch who's been there for you more than me."

Sincere was in his feelings about what I'd said, but I didn't give a damn. I gave his ass nothing but straight facts.

"Whatever, Sincere. Leave!"

"Don't start that shit, Taylor. I told you what was up earlier. I'ma take your nappy headed ass to a club tomorrow, so let that shit go."

"Bye, Sincere."

I gave him my ass to kiss as I walked away from him and back towards the bed. Sincere knew not to say anything else to me. He grabbed his phone and left, again. This time, I stood at the bedroom window for ten minutes making sure he was gone before I made my next move. I yanked my phone off the bed to call Raven back.

"Uh-uh, bitch, don't be calling me back because that gorilla left."

"You almost got us caught, hell. You ready to go?"

"You know I stay ready. Plus, I already told you I'll have my piece with me in the event some bullshit pops off." I rolled my eyes at her, even though she couldn't see me.

It would take her to be ready to shoot somebody over something that's not even worth it. I can't even see why she and Keon were even still together.

"Meet me at Mace's strip club in thirty minutes."

"Tennis shoes and Vaseline, right?"

"Hell, yeah!"

Raven knew what was up. The tennis shoes were there in case we had to run or stomp a bitch. The Vaseline was so nobody could grab ahold of us easily. Plus, it kept you from getting bruises.

"See you shortly, bestie." The call was ended.

Immediately, I took off the t-shirt I lounged around in. After I rubbed Vaseline all over my body, that included my face, I threw on some tights and a t-shirt. I slid on my Chuck Taylors, grabbed my phone and keys, and darted out the door.

****

The strip club was packed as hell. It made me wonder if a big celebrity was in town or something. Raven stood at the front door when I arrived, so I hopped out the car to go join her.

"Took you long enough, hoe."

"Shut up. I said thirty minutes, hell. Nobody told your ass to pull out the bat mobile to get here."

"Whatever, you sure you want to do this?"

"Hell, yeah, I'm sure."

"Come on, then. I know a girl named Mylah that works here. She's going to let us in through the back."

See, I knew Raven's ass would be good for something. I followed her to the back, and a busty chick with a thin waist stood by the back door and motioned for us to hurry.

"If they ask how the hell you got in here, you better play dumb, I can't afford to lose my job." She flat-out said.

We nodded our heads to let her know we understood. But, I pondered over the fact she didn't see that big ass camera over our heads. How the hell could she have missed that? I didn't say shit about it, though. I was on a mission.

"Have you seen my husband?"

I figured I might as well ask her since she worked there.

"Who's your husband?"

"Sincere Griffith."

Her hands flew to her mouth, and red flags went off that let me know that her ass knew something.

"Where is he?" She pointed toward one of the rooms down the hall.

Not waiting for her to say anything else, I headed down the hall to the door she said he was behind.

"Wait, Tay. Let me check first. Maybe he's getting a lap dance." Raven moved in front of me and tried to keep me from going in.

I pushed Raven out of the way and forced my way inside the room. I could've lost it when I saw Sincere sitting back in a chair with some fake ass Tyra Banks wannabe. She was riding his dick while his head was rested on the back of the chair.

"Really, Sincere? This what we doing now? Is this the client your muthafuckin' ass had to meet up with?" I charged at him, swinging like a mad woman.

"What the hell is going on back here?" Mace ran in with a boatload of people behind him.

"Sincere? Devyn? Oh, hell naw, bitch. You were supposed to be my friend. How the fuck is you gonna be in here fuckin' my baby daddy?" One of the women who'd walked in with Mace hollered out. I had no clue who that chick was.

"Wait... What? Nyla are you sure this is your baby's daddy?" The chick named Devyn spoke to whom I now learned was named Nyla.

"What the fuck do you mean? Yes, Sincere is the father of my daughter. I know who I opened my legs to."

The words leaving her mouth crushed my heart. The only reason Sincere didn't want to have a baby with me was because he'd already had a baby with someone else. I'd taken too much from him these past seven years, and I couldn't do it anymore. Enough was a damn nuff.

I dashed back toward Raven, then snatched her purse, causing it to snap from around her. Reaching inside, I removed the gun she was toting. After I aimed straight for Sincere's heart, I let off two rounds before I was tackled to the ground.

Chapter One:
Taylor

"OMG, Taylor, what did you do?" Raven screamed, and it dawned on me that I'd shot somebody.

Never in a million years could someone tell me that I would risk my life over someone that wasn't worth the trouble. How could Sincere betray me like that? Yeah, I knew being with Chaz wasn't the right thing for me to do, but the moment Sincere said he would do better, I left Chaz alone. We were trying to work things out. At least, that's what I thought was supposed to happen, but he had other plans. He never wanted to do right by me. He just wanted me to be at home, and look stupid like I'd done in the past.

"Call the ambulance, somebody." I heard Sincere yell while he stood over the stripper like he was about to give her mouth to mouth. The sound of his voice snapped me out of my thoughts.

"Don't nobody move." I pointed the gun to everyone who stood in the room with us.

My intentions were never to come into the room and shoot anyone, but I wanted to catch Sincere in the act. Deep down, I always knew he wasn't doing right by me, but to see it first-hand, fucked me up. There was no way I could just walk away after I saw him enjoy another bitch's pussy the way he should've only enjoyed mine.

"Get away from her." I turned the gun back to Sincere. "Next time, I won't miss," I assured him, even though I knew there wouldn't be a next time.

Sincere slowly moved away from the stripper. What bothered me the most was when the other stripper revealed she had a baby by Sincere. All those years, I discussed us having children, it was always something. "I'm not ready for kids. Let's wait until we turn thirty. I don't want kids to distract us from each other," and whatever other lie his ass came up with to make me feel as though we didn't need kids. The whole time he lied to me, he was busy playing house with the next bitch.

"I'm sorry, Tay. I didn't mean for any of this to happen."

"No, you meant for it to happen. You just didn't mean for me to find out about the shit. Now, you're going to pay for all the pain you've caused me."

Sincere dropped to his knees, begging and pleading with me to not kill him. As bad as I wanted to pull the trigger and remove him from his miserable life, I couldn't. The tears formed in my eyes began to blur my vision. How could I be so stupid? How could I not see what had gone on before my eyes?

"Baby, I swear we can work this out. We don't have to tell the police you did this. We can go home and act like none of this happened." Sincere spoke as he crawled on his knees toward me.

"You move one more inch and I'll shoot your fuckin' kneecaps off." I roared, loudly.

"Give me the gun, Tay. This isn't like you. You have entirely too much to lose." Raven came toward me and tried her best to remove the gun from my hands.

As badly as I didn't want to let her take the gun, I had no choice. Being that the stripper chick was on the floor profusely coughing, I had no choice but to allow them to call the ambulance. My life was ruined all because I couldn't walk away from Sincere a long time ago.

I handed Raven the gun, but I couldn't take my eyes off Sincere. I stared a hole through his soul. I swear, if looks could kill, his ass would've been killed at least twenty times by now. The way I was looking at him, must've had him scared to move because even after Raven removed the gun from my hand, Sincere never moved from the spot he was in.

"Tay, lo-." He spoke, but I threw my hand up to stop him.

At that point, there was nothing left for Sincere and I to discuss. When he walked out of the home we shared to go screw another bitch, he made the decision to end our marriage. This time, I was going to stick to it. There was no turning back or working it out. I'd given more than enough of myself to that man in an attempt to work things out, but this truly proved our relationship wasn't salvageable.

"If I were you, I'd leave while I had the chance," Raven stated before she ran toward Sincere and kicked him between the legs.

Sincere weltered over in pain and rolled around on the floor while he held his dick in his hands. I wanted to laugh so bad, but I couldn't. It wasn't the time or the place. I made a mental note to thank Raven later for what she did.

"Devyn, are you okay?" Nyla briskly walked to where Devyn was laid on the floor.

"Give me a break, she was only shot in the shoulder and the shit went straight through." Mylah nonchalantly spoke before she rolled her eyes. "Give the bitch a band-aid, she'll be alright." She muttered as she left the room.

"Well, fuck you, too, bitch." Devyn sat up and looked around the room. "I can't believe you shot me. This shit hurts. Somebody call the police."

"Shut up, Devyn. There ain't no need to be calling the police. You're not dead and you sure as hell ain't dying." Sincere called himself speaking up for me.

"I don't care, she could've killed me. I want her arrested."

"No, I said no police. We're going to say this was an accident. She wasn't even aiming for you. You got your dumbass in the way. That's what you get for trying to blackmail me." Sincere countered.

Hearing he had been blackmailed was a shocker and new to me. What reason did she have to blackmail him? Did she know about the baby with that Nyla person?

All kinds of questions invaded my mind as I tried my best to fit the pieces to this messed up puzzle together.

"It's not what you think." Sincere reached out to me, causing me to step back.

There was no way I would allow Sincere to touch me again. Not after what I'd just witnessed him doing and certainly not after I'd heard he had a baby behind my back.

"Taylor, let's go home and talk about this."

"There's nothing to discuss, now let's get this bitch to the hospital." Raven stepped in to defend me.

She must've gotten tired of hearing Sincere's fake pleas, just as I had.

"Raven, I'm so sick of you sticking your nose where it doesn't belong. This has absolutely nothing to do with you. What happens between my wife and me, is our fuckin' business. If you were so concerned about your relationship with Keon as you are with what Tay and I have going on, then maybe that nigga wouldn't have been cheating on your ass."

"How the hell you know what my man doing? He ain't nothing like your dog ass."

"You're a damn lie. Besides, I went through Devyn's phone when I stayed the night with her and saw texts between her and Keon. I knew it was your nigga because I compared the number in her phone to the one I have saved in my phone for him."

My mouth dropped open listening to what Sincere had just informed Raven. She stood there for a moment in complete and utter silence. What she did next fucked me up. I never saw it coming.

Raven very calmly inched her way over to Sincere. She studied the room a minute, then refocused her attention on him.

"What did you just say?"

"You heard exactly what I said. Don't act like you don't know what I'm talking about. Keon fuckin' anything walking around here with a cat between their legs. He doesn't even give a damn what they look like. I guess anything was better than being with your dry pussy ass." Sincere taunted Raven then had the nerve to laugh about it.

What the hell did he do that for? Raven raised the gun in her hand and bashed Sincere upside the head with it. I knew I should've tried to stop her, but I felt as though he deserved everything he was getting. Had he left well enough alone, he wouldn't be in that predicament.

I stood back and observed as Raven got the upper-hand on Sincere. With the amount of blood that leaked from his head, you would've thought she would've cared enough to stop. Raven must've thought, *fuck that,* as she continued to beat his ass with the gun. The only thing Sincere could do was lie down on the floor and try to cover his head, with his pussy ass. It was all fun and games until the gun went off.

I didn't care to see what happened at that point. Immediately, I jumped to the ground and prayed no one else got hurt.

Chapter Two:
Sincere

"You fucking bitch, I can't believe you shot me," I growled and tried my best to regain enough energy to beat Raven's ass.

The crazy bitch attacked me all because I gave her the 4-1-1 on her man. How the hell she gonna get mad at me for keeping it real with her? If anything, she shoulda been home whooping up on that nigga.

As bad as I wanted to beat her ass, I could barely move. My leg was in excruciating pain from the gunshot wound. She shot me in my thigh close to my groin area. The only thing I kept thinking was, *Thank God it wasn't my dick.*

"Help me, Tay," I called out to my wife.

Taylor instantly jumped up from the floor to come to my aid. Yeah, y'all can get mad all you want to, but Taylor knew what the deal was. No matter what the hell I did wrong, she had to make sure I was good and she had to make sure our relationship was good. Why the hell do you think I do the things I do? All because I knew that she would come running back as if nothing ever happened just like the rest of you women do.

"Raven? Why'd you shoot him?"

"It was an accident, Tay. Why the hell do you care anyways? He hasn't done anything but hurt you ever since y'all got together."

"I know, but I didn't think you would shoot him."

"How many times do you want me to say it was an accident. However, I don't feel an ounce of remorse for it. He deserved everything he got and so much more."

"Fuck you, bitch," I blurted out, not giving a damn how she felt.

So, what if I were wrong for telling the truth about her man, don't y'all think she supposed to know? I mean, wouldn't you want to know? I thought I was helping her out. I couldn't help, but smirk. I knew exactly what I was doing when I said what I said to her. She needed to feel the same way I was feeling. Shit, don't they say, "Sweep around your own front door before you sweep around mine." She should've been taking heed to those words.

"Y'all, we have to call the ambulance. Two people have been shot," Nyla whimpered.

Glimpsing at her, I wanted to slap the dog piss out of her for disclosing the fact we shared a child. That was something I wanted to tell her. Actually, it was something I needed to tell her, but that was ruined all because Nyla didn't know how to keep her trap shut.

"I don't need you saying shit else. You've caused more than enough damage. Don't you think?"

"What the hell did I do?"

"You came in here running your mouth, that's what you did."

"What difference does it make? You're not about to keep denying our daughter. Then, you had the nerve to be at my job, sleeping with one of the bitches I was kicking it with. You don't see the problem with that?"

"Would you two shut the hell up? There's nothing you can say, Sincere, that will make me change my mind about this marriage being over. While it would've benefited me if Raven would've killed your ass when she shot you, I can't do anything about that now."

"This marriage isn't over until I say it's over and if you try to leave me, there will be a lot of consequences for it."

"You don't fuckin' threaten me, Sincere. You obviously made up your mind who you wanted to be with when you had a baby with her."

"I don't want that bitch. If I did, I would've been left you, but I'm not going anywhere. This marriage is for better or worse. You remember that? When we took those vows, we were supposed to stick to them. Failure isn't an option in this relationship."

I meant everything I was saying to her. The only way for her to get out of this marriage was if either one of us died and I wasn't planning to die anytime soon.

It was clear Taylor didn't like anything I had to say by the facial expression she gave me. She stood to walk away from me. I called out to her, but she wouldn't turn around. She simply kept walking out the door, but not before hollering out that she would meet us at the hospital.

After Taylor finally left the room, Nyla was able to call the ambulance to come for Devyn and me. She walked between the both of us to make sure neither one of us needed anything. Noticing that she was spending a little more time checking on Devyn than me, I had to ask her what was going on.

"What's the problem, Ny? Why are you acting like you got a problem with a nigga?"

"Because I do. I shouldn't have ever messed with you. You ain't bout shit." She sneered while rolling her eyes at me.

"What the hell are you talking about? I ain't did shit to your loopy ass."

"So, you didn't just tell your wife that you didn't want me? That's funny, seeing as though every time you in this pussy, you talk about how you want to marry me, so we can be a family for our daughter."

"You've got to be kidding me. Did you even hear yourself? The only time I say the shit is when I'm in the pussy. Bitch, you don't realize good pussy will have you saying all kinds of bullshit because that's exactly what I was doing." I corrected her thinking.

Why should I sit there and allow her to think we had a chance to be together when we didn't? She should've known from the jump I wouldn't leave my wife for her or anybody else, so she needed to get over it.

It took the ambulance what seemed like forever to get there. Everyone in the room decided we would act like some people came in to rob us and Devyn and I were shot. At least that was the plan, until the police came in, and asked all kinds of questions. They even asked for the surveillance videos the club kept, but luckily, Mace told them that the cameras were just for show. Everything was running smoothly until Nyla became too antsy.

"She did it. His wife came in here and shot everybody. Look at all this damn blood."

"Girl, if you don't stop lying, I'ma beat your ass." I hollered as I listened to her blab to the police.

"Excuse me, sir, we're trying to get her statement." An officer addressed me.

"I don't give a fuck what you're trying to do. That bitch ain't doing shit but lying. How the hell you got a whole group of people telling you what really happened and a bald-headed, no edge having, wig wearing, pussy smelling, cactus face bitch telling you a lie, and you ready to roll with it?" I was furious. "If you really want to know the truth, Nyla is pissed off because I stopped giving her the dick, so she's trying to do everything in her power to get at my wife, but I'm not about to let that shit go down like that."

"Nigga, please! Ain't nobody worried about you or that lil ass dick you got. Hell, I had to fake most of my orgasms. The only reason I still fuck with you is because we have a child and you keep us laced in money; money that belongs to your wife, if I might add."

As she continued to run her mouth, I did everything I could to get on my feet. My leg was hurting something serious, but that didn't matter to me. I was determined to shut Nyla up once and for all. She talked so much shit because she thought I couldn't do anything to her, but she had another thing coming.

Mace raced over to help me up since I shooed the paramedics away. "You need to chill out homie and let these people help you before you do more damage to your leg."

"I will in just a minute, I need to do something first."

When I was completely on my feet, I moved towards Nyla to see what else she said to the officer. I listened to her tell them the whole story from start to finish, and it made me angry. I couldn't let that fly, so I lunged at her in a way that would appear as though I'd fallen. Everything was working in my favor. I knew I was going to be able to lay hands on her until she took a few steps back and I landed on the floor. I wallowed in pain and prayed the Lord would just end my life. Anything was better than the pain I was feeling. Not only was I about to lose my wife, but my side bitches had stepped out of line, and all my secrets were out of the bag. Could this shit get any worse for me?

Chapter Three:
Devyn

Tonight had been one hell of a night. I got shot, lost my job, and didn't get the money I intended on getting from blackmailing Sincere. Not to mention, I had to sit at the hospital for hours, waiting for someone to come in and talk to me.

"Hello, Ms. Smith, how are you feeling?" The doctor asked as soon as he walked in.

"I'm fine, sir. I'm just ready to go home. Do you know how much longer I have here?"

"You'll be able to go home as soon as we're done checking you out, which shouldn't be too much longer. The nurse told me that you reported being pregnant when you got here, so we need to also check to make sure the baby is fine as well."

"How long is that shit going to take? I'm ready to go. I have shit to do." I fussed at him, knowing he wasn't the one I needed to be mad at. I was the reason I was in the situation I was in, but it felt good being able to take my aggression out on someone else.

"I can assure you it won't take long at all. Don't you want to make sure your baby is okay?"

"To be honest with you, Doc, I really don't give a damn. The way my life is right now, I don't need any more damn kids." I spat, truthfully.

"Well, however you chose to handle it when you leave here is totally up to you, but while you're in my care, I'll have to check both you and the baby out."

After the doctor finished nursing my wound, it didn't take long for an ultrasound tech to walk in with an ultrasound machine to make sure everything with the baby looked fine.

"Okay, Ms. Smith, I'm about to put some gel on your stomach, it's going to be a little cold." The tech informed me before she pulled out a white tube and squeezed a lubricant on my stomach. She placed a transducer probe on my stomach and used it to rub the gel in before she kept it steady enough for us to see the baby.

"Aww... There goes your little peanut right there and the heartbeat seems to be normal."

"How far along am I?" I only asked because I thought it was too soon to hear the heartbeat.

"From the measurements, the sound of the heartbeat, and from the dates you gave regarding your last menstrual cycle, I'd say you're about eight weeks pregnant, but the doctor will look at the images and confirm what I just told you."

Once the tech completed the ultrasound, she printed the pictures of the baby, then handed them to me. I threw them on top of my purse without giving them a second thought. If the information she gave me regarding the due date was accurate, then I knew for sure Keon was the father. That nigga had a whole girlfriend at home, so I knew his ass wasn't going to step up and do what he needed to do for our child as Chaz did for Cassie. The thought of having him in my life for the rest of my life kind of fucked with me, so I didn't know what to think of all this.

The doctor returned shortly after the tech to confirm the information that she had given me. While I wasn't too happy about the situation, I was glad I still had enough time to have an abortion, if I decided that would be my next move.

"Well, since everything is fine with the baby, can I go home now?"

"Yes, you may go home. All I ask is that you take care of yourself and try to relax. I'm shocked you didn't miscarry the baby from all the stress that was just put on your body. That right there was a sign that there may be a reason for all of this."

The more I listened to the doctor talk, the more I considered the possibility that he could be right, but I still wasn't trying to hear that shit. There was no way I could have the baby and I'm pretty convinced I won't.

As for Keon, I don't think I could even be mad at him for the way he acted towards me. All those years, he tried to love me, but I continuously pushed him away. He didn't have the amount of money I needed to continue to live my lavish lifestyle. Now, I'm sitting here too scared to tell him that I'm pregnant by him.

Once I was ready to leave the hospital, I called Keon to see if there was any way he could pick me up. Of course, after I dialed his number, he had the nerve to send me straight to voicemail. That left me with no choice but to call Chaz. I shook my head as I thought about what he would say when he found out I was at the hospital and why. I knew I was going to be left with a major headache once he chewed my head off for putting myself in that kind of situation. I had no choice but to tell him the truth because if I didn't, I knew it would eventually come out and lying to him would only tarnish what little relationship we had. Clearing my head, I dialed his number. Luckily, he picked up on the third ring.

"What's up, Devyn?" Chaz quizzed sounding groggy.

"Hey, baby daddy. I need you to pick me up from Cooper Hospital."

"What the hell are you doing at the hospital, Devyn?"

"I was shot, Chaz, but I don't want to talk about that right now. If you come pick me up, I'll tell you everything once you get here." After responding to him, I hurried to hang the phone up before he could say another word. I knew that when he arrived, he was going to cuss my ass out.

As I paced back and forth, I tried to come up with different scenarios to give Chaz that would lead him to think that someone else was to blame for this mess, but I couldn't think of anything. I didn't want to disappoint him and let him know that I was working at the strip club again, but I really had no choice. That in itself, was more than enough information to get my head chopped off. But, then again, I got fired anyways, so maybe he wouldn't be so upset to learn that I wasn't going back.

It took twenty minutes before Chaz arrived. He stormed into my room as if he were on a mission.

"Devyn, what the fuck happened to you?" Chaz asked with sadness in his eyes.

"I'm okay, Chaz. Some crazy ass bitch came in the strip club and shot it up." He looked at me with a side eye.

"What the hell were you doing at the strip club? I thought you had to work tonight?"

"Chaz, I was at work. I started working at the strip club again a couple of weeks ago," I confessed in almost a whisper.

"So, did somebody really come shoot the club up or did they come there to shoot your hoe ass for messing with their husband?"

"Fuck you, Chaz! Just take me the hell home and you don't have to worry about me asking you to do anything else for me."

"Devyn, shut the hell up because you always need me to do something for you. Now, hurry up and get your ass up and let's go. You so damn hard-headed, working in a fucking strip club." He fussed while he walked out the door.

He was so mad he didn't even bother to check to see if I was okay enough to walk. Once we made it out of the hospital and into his car, I was sick of the quietness.

"What did you expect me to do, Chaz? You stopped giving me money and I had bills to pay."

"Get a real fucking job, Devyn. Shit, the whole time I was taking care of your ass you could've went to school or something. It's time for you to get your life straight, ma. I would never want to keep Cassie away from you, but if you don't get your shit together, I'm gon' have to. What would've happened if you died in that strip club tonight? I would've had to explain to my baby that her momma wasn't coming back, and that's not no shit I'm ever trying to do." Chaz admitted.

When he finished reading my ass, I felt like shit, and tears ran down my face. Chaz was right, it was time for me to get my shit together; if not for myself, at least for Cassie. The ride home took forever and I was in a lot of pain, on top of the heartbreak. I was so in my feelings that I didn't wanna do shit but lie down and go to sleep. Once I made it inside the house, Chaz left, so I laid on my couch and turned the TV on. I heard my phone go off, alerting me that I had a text message.

Keon: *What's up, ma?*

Me: *Hey, Keon, what's up with you?*

Keon: *I've been missing you. Can I come over tonight?*

Me: *Sure, why not? We need to talk anyway.*

Keon: *I'll be there shortly.*

I knew if I would've said anything about his girlfriend he wouldn't have come, so I figured I'd talk to him when he got here. That shit still blew my mind about him trying to commit to me know that he had a whole girlfriend, but what could I say about it, when I was fuckin' other niggas, too.

The pain in my shoulder started to come again and I knew Tylenol wasn't going to relieve it, but it was all the doctor said I could take due to the pregnancy. Then, I thought about the fact that I wasn't going to keep the baby, and headed straight for my medicine cabinet, and grabbed a Percocet. I knew that shit would put me straight to sleep. I shot Keon a message to let him know I would leave a key under the doormat, so he could let himself in.

After the text was sent and Keon replied, *okay,* I put the key under the mat like I said I would, then headed to the kitchen and grabbed a bottle of water. With the Perc in one hand and the bottle of water in the other, I headed straight back to the couch in the living room. Finding something good to watch on TV, I plopped down on the couch and took the pill. It wasn't too long after that, that I drifted off to sleep.

Chapter Four:
Chaz

I was fed up with Devyn and in complete awe that she took her ass back to the strip club to work after I told her ass not to. We've had plenty of talks about her working there and she promised me that she would never go back. Of course, she lied to me like she usually does. Out of all the women in the world, I had to have a baby by one of those chicks who didn't know how to be a mother and do right to save their lives.

Since it was still kind of early, I figured I would swing by my bar to see how things were going and possibly grab a few drinks. I didn't drink often, but tonight, I needed something to calm my damn nerves.

After speeding down the highway, I made it to the bar in record breaking time. My anger was on one hundred, and I was glad I didn't get pulled over. Parking in my usual spot and jumping out my car, I headed straight inside of my establishment.

"Yo', boss man, what up homie?"

"Hey, Levi, what's up, bro? Can you tell Toya to send me a bottle of Henny up to my office?"

"Alright, boss, I'll have her bring it right up." Levi paused, then looked at me before he proceeded to speak again. "You look like you need to talk, so I'll just grab that for you."

I should've known Levi was gon' come see what was up with me. That was my go to person when shit got real in my life. Other than my parents, I didn't talk to anyone, but Levi.

Once I made it inside my office, I walked straight to my desk and turned the camera on. The place wasn't too packed tonight, but it was early, so I hoped business would pick up in a couple hours.

"So, what's good wit' you, boss?" Levi inquired when he strolled into my office toting a bottle of Henny and two shot glasses.

"You already know what's wrong with me, my nigga."

"What Devyn ass do now?"

"Tell me why her ass is back working at the damn strip club."

"You're joking, right?"

"Hell no, I'm not joking. And that's not the worse part. Tell me why her ass ended up getting shot tonight."

"I heard something about a club getting shot up, but I didn't know Devyn was the person that got shot."

"Well, what did you hear?"

The shit Levi said had really peaked my interest. I knew Devyn's ass wouldn't tell me the truth about what happened, but I knew Levi wouldn't hold shit back.

"From what I heard, some nigga's wife went up there and caught him with a stripper in the back or some shit like that. They said the wife was so angry, she set it off in that bitch. Damn, it had to be Devyn the wife was after since she was the one who got shot. That's some wild shit, boss."

"See, I specifically asked Devyn was somebody's wife coming for her and she fuckin' lied to me."

"Boss, the story I got was just hearsay. It might not even be true, but some cat did come in here, a little while ago, and said they shut the strip club down. He was drunk and Toya wouldn't serve him, so he left."

"Naw, Levi, that shit's probably true."

Levi opened the Henny and poured me a shot. I downed it without giving it a second thought and asked him to pour me another one. By the time I took the third shot, I had started to feel nice. I looked at the monitors to see what was going on at the bar and noticed business had picked up. More people had started to come in.

"Levi, I think you need to head on down to the bar. It's starting to get crowded down there."

"Damn, already? It was just empty in this bitch." Levi expressed while he stared at the monitor with me.

He paused for and minute, because something caught his eye, then, stood to leave my office.

"What's up, man? What are you looking at?"

"Your girl walked in. I haven't seen her in and while and I bet she's here to see you."

I hadn't seen Taylor in a while either, and I promised myself I wasn't gon' be bothered with her. All the back and forth shit she did between me and her husband, wasn't working for me. I ain't gon' lie and say I don't think about her constantly, but she ain't gon' play with my feelings.

"Tell her to come see me when you get down there."

I knew having her coming up here wasn't a good idea because I was feeling the effect of the alcohol, but hey, I didn't give a damn.

I took another shot and waited for her to make her appearance. A little knock was heard, then my door opened. Once Taylor came inside, I could tell something was wrong, and baby girl needed a hug.

"Lock the door and come here," I said, then stood up and walked over to her. She ran right into my arms and the tears fell from her face. I pulled back and looked into her eyes. I could see she was shaken up about something.

"What's wrong, ma?"

"Everything is wrong, Chaz. I should've not gone back to him. Today could've gone all wrong for me. I could've been arrested for the rest of my life behind my actions." I knew she needed to talk, but at this time, and the way I was feeling, I didn't want to hear her babbling on.

Interrupting her from speaking, I kissed her lips and just like I knew she would, she put her tongue in my mouth. We kissed each other hard and rough. I guess we both wanted each other bad as hell. I picked her up, then walked her over to my desk. I put her down while I removed everything. Once I was finished, I turned around and Taylor stood in front of me naked as the day she was born.

Looking at her beautiful body, my mouth started to water, so I scooped her up, and she wrapped her legs around my waist. As if it were a natural reaction, we kissed each other again. By then, my dick was standing at attention and ready to slide right in her, but I wasn't ready to do that just yet. I wanted to taste her first. She smelled just as good as she did the last time I saw her. After I stared at her precious pearl for a minute, I dived right in, flicking my tongue in a fast motion on her clit.

"Oh, my, God, Chaz! I'm about to cum... I'm about to cum..." Taylor expressed loudly enough for my neighbors to hear.

After I made her bust her first nut, I unbuttoned my pants and let them drop to the floor. Then, I picked Taylor up and she wrapped her legs around me once again. Walking her over to the wall in the corner of my office, I slid right into her. I bit down on my bottom lip, enjoying the feeling of her wetness.

Taylor was nice and tight, just the way I liked it. I gave her long, hard, and deep strokes that sent us both spiraling into ecstasy. Taylor and I didn't waste our time doing too much talking. All that was heard throughout my office were our moans, the sounds of me going in and out of her wetness, and our skin, slapping against each other. Her pussy muscles were starting to tighten up on my dick, so I knew she was about to cum. I could actually feel my nut building up, too, so I knew I was ready to cum as well.

"I'm about to cum, baby, you ready to bust this nut with me?" I asked Taylor while staring into her eyes.

I was still giving her those long, hard strokes.

"Yessssssssssssssss Chazzzzzzzzz, I'm cuminnnnnn!" Taylor screamed.

"Let that shit go, ma! I'm cumin, too."

After we both finished, I felt my legs get wobbly, and I couldn't move. I had to stand still and lean her up against the wall, so I wouldn't drop her. Once I got my equilibrium back on track, I carried Taylor to the bathroom to give her some privacy. After I cleaned myself up, and put my clothes back on, I sat on the couch and waited for her to come back. I didn't want to hear what happened between her and that fuck boy, but the least I could do was listen to her vent after the good ass pussy she had just given me.

"I'm sorry, Chaz. I just came in here, telling you all my problems without asking you how you were doing." Taylor walked over to me after she'd put her clothes on and sat on my lap.

"You good, ma. I've been going through some shit of my own today but seeing you and that sex session we just had made me feel a whole lot better. Thank you, baby, I needed that."

"Thank you, too. I needed that as well. So, what're your plans for the rest of the night?"

"I wasn't doing shit but drinking my problems away."

"Well, how about we grab that bottle of Henny and go back to your house. At least that way, we can drink our problems away together." Taylor suggested.

"That sounds like a plan to me. It could be a Henny-Thing-Goes type of night." I responded while smiling at Taylor.

Chapter Five:

Raven

I swear all niggas be on some shit, which was part of the reason I stayed single. Keon waited until I got good and attached to his ass to do me dirty. I swear I'm so sick of that shit. I cook, I clean, and I fuck that nigga on a regular. I see why my mama and grandma always told me not to do wife shit until I became a wife. I should've listened. Now, look at my ass, sitting here on the couch broken hearted once again.

Hearing a knock on my door, followed by it being unlocked, I knew it was Keon. He hit the light switch to turn them on. When I could be seen, I noticed him staring at me like a deer stuck in headlights before he headed straight for the couch where I as propped up.

"Baby, why are you sitting in here with the lights off?"

"Get your shit and get the fuck out my house, and I mean grab everything, so you won't have to come back. You really should go check on your bitch, Devyn, to make sure her ass ain't dead." He walked toward me.

"If you come any closer, I'll shoot your mutha fuckin' ass, then take my ass upstairs and go to bed. Fuck with me if you want to, and watch what happens. Like I said, the first time, get your shit and get out my house, and if you take too long, I'll be sure to come up there and make you move faster."

Keon didn't say shit, he just headed upstairs and did as he was told. I knew he wished he'd brought his gun inside with him, but too damn bad. See, I knew my ass was crazy, and there ain't no telling what would go wrong if we got into a fight. I always made him think I was scared of guns, so he left it in his car when he stayed at my crib.

My name is Raven Nickerson and I'm twenty-eight years old. I was born and raised in Camden, New Jersey. I grew up right in the hood. My mother was a prostitute, and my pops was a street nigga. He taught me everything I knew about shooting a gun, slangin' dope, robbing niggas, and hiding bodies. Of course, he didn't want me to live that type of life, so he made sure I went to school. I was almost done going to school for Nursing with a BSN. That's a Bachelor's of Science in nursing, in case you didn't know.

Taylor and I were going to school for the same thing until Sincere's dumb ass happened. I can't stand his stupid ass. I kinda wished I would've killed his ass tonight. I wasn't even worried about going to jail because I knew plenty of people that could dispose of his body without a trace.

While I was in deep thought, Keon came down the stairs, dragging two trash bags full of shit. He looked at me with pity in his eyes. I knew he was about to say something, so I continued to look at him. I wanted him to say whatever was on his mind, then get the fuck outta my shit.

"I'm sorry, Raven. I didn't mean to hurt you, baby."

"Keon, save that shit for somebody that gives a damn because I don't. Now, get the fuck out before I shoot you in the dick you couldn't keep in your pants. And don't call me, because I ain't forgiving you. It only takes one time to fuck with my heart, then it's a wrap. If you ever step foot on my property again, I'll blow your fucking head off."

Instead of responding, Keon dropped his head and headed towards the door. When I looked at the door, I thought of something else.

"Oh, and Keon??" I called out to him.

"Yes…" He enthusiastically looked back at me as if he thought I'd changed my mind.

"Leave my key on the table on your way out."

A look of defeat was evident on his face as he dropped my key on the coffee table and continued on out the door.

Once he'd exited the house, I said a silent prayer that I would never see him again. I rushed to hop up and lock everything up after he left to avoid him coming back in without permission, then headed to my bedroom to cry my heart out. Today would be the last day I'd allow myself to cry over a nigga because I was done with love.

My phone went off in my pocket. Pulling it out, I noticed I had a text from Levi.

Levi: Hey, sweetie, what's up with you?

Me: Nothing's up with me. I'm not doing too good, but I'll be ok. I thought I'd never hear from you.

Levi: *Why would you think that. I asked you for your number, didn't I?*

Me: *I don't know, sometimes niggas play.*

Levi: *I ain't no kid baby girl, I don't play games. So, what you been up to?*

Me: *Nothing much, just going to school.*

Levi: *That's cool and all, but when you gone let me take you out?*

Me: *I just got out of a relationship. I don't need to be moving on so soon.*

Levi: *I'm not asking you to marry me, sweetheart. I just wanna take you out to eat or something like that.*

Me: *Okay, well, how about I hit you back tomorrow?*

Levi: *That's cool as long as you don't forget about me.*

Levi didn't seem like my type, but maybe, something different was what I needed since the drug dealing, street niggas were getting old. He seemed like the working type that didn't do much besides work. That life seemed a little boring. Maybe, that's why I couldn't find a good dude that kept his dick in his pants; because all I wanted was a street nigga.

Once I was done texting Levi, I laid my ass down in my bed and took a nap, but I was awakened by a loud ass knock on my door. They had to be knocking hard as hell for me to hear that shit all the way up in my room.

"Who the fuck is knocking on my door like that?" I expressed to myself before I hopped up and headed down to my front door with a mean scowl on my face, ready to cuss whoever was at my door out. That was until I pulled it open and was face to face with someone I never expected.

"Hello, ma'am. Are you Raven Nickerson?" I already knew what they were there for, but I couldn't believe Sincere's fuckin' bitch ass. Next time, I ain't letting his pussy ass live. He's going to get one straight to the dome.

"Yes, I'm Raven Nickerson. How may I help you, officer?"

"Well Ms. Nickerson, you're under arrest for shooting Sincere Griffith. He's pressing charges against you, so I have to take you in."

With no reason to put up a fight, I just turned around and let them do their job. When I called my dad to come pick me up, I knew he was going to have a fit. Sincere was a sucka ass bitch, and I didn't understand how Taylor still dealt with his punk ass. He probably got mad because she didn't meet his sorry ass at the hospital. I'm sure he thought it was my doing, but that shit had nothing to do with me. She actually told me she wasn't going up there to see his ass because she was going to go see Chaz. I was happy as shit to hear her say that. My BFF deserved better than Sincere and I hoped tonight she realized that.

It wasn't long before I was handcuffed and ready to go. "Can y'all please make sure my door is locked?"

"Yes, ma'am, we will."

I guess they were being nice because I wasn't resisting. To be honest, I wasn't trying to fight because I was good and tired. All I wanted to do was lay down and get some sleep, so this day would be over with. Hopefully, my dad will be to the jail to get me out first thing in the morning. It ain't like I ain't never spent a night in jail before, so I knew I'd be fine.

Chapter Six:

Keon

For the life of me, I couldn't figure out how the hell Raven found out about me fuckin' with Devyn. Yeah, I talked a lot of shit to Devyn about wanting to leave Raven and be with her, but the more I thought about it, the more I realized how big of a fuckin' fool I would be.

Devyn was the type of chick that you just couldn't please. No matter how much money I gave her, how many bills I paid for her, how good I dicked her down, or how many times I allowed her to belittle me, she treated me like straight garbage. I knew it was because I wasn't clocking major bucks like Chaz, but damn, a nigga deserved to get some type of credit for the shit he did.

Raven, on the other hand, was a completely different breed. She appreciated me for whatever I did for her and even encouraged me to get my life together when I didn't feel I could. She did things for me that I've never had anyone do for me, like show me, love. My own mother didn't even give me that. Maybe, that's why I didn't know how to appreciate having a good woman in my life. Now, I've messed that up.

Devyn hit me up, wanting me to come over and talk to her. The only thing I wanted to talk about was leaving her ass alone so I could make things right with Raven. I hoped she wasn't about to come at me on some bullshit like most women do when you tell them that you not fuckin' with them no more. You know how they be claiming that they pregnant or that they gonna kill themselves; ain't nobody got time for that shit. I should've left her ass alone a long time ago, but her head game was fiyah and the way she rode my dick was unfuckin' believable. You'd have to be a nigga to understand that shit.

Arriving at Devyn's crib, I sat outside in the car for a minute to gather my thoughts. I didn't know how she would react to me telling her that I didn't want her, but she was going to have to deal with it. I wasn't in the business of being anybody's secret or money pot and that's exactly what Devyn wanted.

Finally finding the nerve to step out the car, I went straight to her front door, reached under the mat, and grabbed the key. With the key in my hand, I unlocked her door and walked inside, but I wanted to turn around and go back outside since the damn house was fuckin' filthy. As good of a place she had, and as nice as it was decked out, you would think her ass would try to keep the shit clean, right? Hell no. I saw then, why her baby daddy ain't want shit to do with her.

When I wanted to be down for Devyn, I overlooked everything that was wrong with her. Now that I can see the grass wasn't greener on the other side, I see every fault her ass had, starting with the fact that she doesn't appreciate me. Let me not even get started on how fucked up of a mother she was. I wouldn't want her ass to watch my dog, so I knew damn well I wouldn't be able to deal with her raising a child of mine. The more and more I thought about it, the more I missed everything about Raven. This may sound sappy as hell, but I'm so Raven!

"Devyn," I called out to her as I trodden through her nasty ass house, trying to find her.

Walking inside her bedroom, I saw Devyn sleeping. She looked so peaceful. She almost looked like an angel, but that wouldn't change my mind about what I was there to do. Wanting to get the talk over with, I went over to the bed and shook her. It seemed like it took forever for her to open her eyes. When she did, she looked very groggy, and her eyes had a glossy film to them.

"Aye, ma, you good?" I asked, concerned about the way she looked; even her demeanor was off.

Devyn laid in the bed naked. That wasn't anything concerning because she always slept in her birthday suit. What was alarming to me was the bandage on her arm. She didn't tell me anything had happened to her, so the bandage caught me off guard.

"Don't stare at it like that. The doctor said it would heal in no time." She spoke, causing me to refocus my attention on her.

"What the hell happened to you?"

"Some crazy bitch came in the club trying to shoot that bitch up. I just so happened to be the person that took the bullet."

I was shocked by the information she had given me, but I didn't say anything. I wanted to wait until she told me the complete story before I overreacted.

"Are you listening to me?"

"Yeah, I hear you, ma. I'm waiting for you to finish telling me the story."

"I am finished. That's the end of it. A crazy bitch shot me."

"Devyn, people don't just walk inside of clubs and start shooting for no reason; especially not women, so what aren't you telling me?"

She had to take me for a fuckin' fool. Devyn was definitely keeping something from me.

Devyn sat up on the bed with tears in her eyes. In the past, I would allow her to play me to the left by starting that crying shit, and I would just let the shit go, but not this time. Her ass was going to tell me the real story if she wanted me to show any ounce of concern for her ass. I was so frustrated by the entire situation that I began pacing back and forth, putting more wear and tear on her carpet.

"Sit down, Keon. You're making me nervous."

"You think I give a damn about you being nervous? Hell no, I don't. Now tell me what the hell happened."

"Promise you won't get mad at me."

"I ain't promising you shit, now spit out the damn story." I was mad before she even told me the real deal.

"Baby, just hear me out. I fucked up, okay. I was fuckin' with this dude and didn't know he was married, but that was before our time."

The way she spoke had let me know her ass was lying. She wouldn't even make eye contact with me.

"You think you talking to a retarded nigga or something? I ain't no damn idiot, Devyn. Ain't no bitch bout to come after you because of a man you fucked with a long time ago. You had to have still been fuckin' with him. Stop lying to me, Devyn!" My voice was raised and I was yelling louder than I probably should've been.

Devyn reached out for me, but I moved back. Each time she tried to walk up to me, I pushed her back. I didn't want her touching me, period. Knowing I needed to leave before I did something irrational, I decided to nix the conversation I was planning to have with her. It wasn't worth the trouble.

As I prepared to leave, I took one last look at Devyn. While I no longer desired to have an adult conversation with her childish ass, I couldn't leave without getting some shit off my chest. In my mind, it was going to be the last time I would be in her presence. It was either say what I needed to say now, or not say anything at all, and that wasn't the type of nigga I was. I always kept shit a buck no matter what was going on.

"I'ma say this as nicely as I can because I don't like fuckin' with hoes, so sit your ass there and listen. The shit we had is over. You were never worth me losing my girl over. No matter how much I tried to be a rock for you, and support your ungrateful ass, nothing was ever enough. At this point, don't call me, don't text me, and stay the fuck away from my social media accounts with your stalking ass. I don't even want you to think about me."

"What about the baby?"

"What damn baby?" I spat knowing she was trying to hit me with some dumb shit.

"I'm pregnant Keon."

"What does that have to do with me?"

"It's yours." She called herself confirming to me that I was indeed the father of her child, but I wasn't trying to hear that. I didn't even believe any of the shit she said. "What about the baby, Keon?" She asked again like I was supposed to get excited about a seed that I'm sure wasn't mine.

"What about it? That shit ain't mine. If you fuckin' me and that other nigga, ain't no telling who else been off in that shit. Apparently, Donald Trump been in that bitch cuz it's evident somebody knocked your walls down. Stay the fuck away from me. And you might as well dead that baby shit because I don't want shit to do with you or it." I didn't give her a chance to respond before I exited.

While the shit I said to her might have sounded harsh, I meant every word. The day I met her ass, I should've kept walking. All she did was ruin my life. Being involved with her wasn't even worth it.

As I prepared to get back inside my car, my phone rang. Not bothering to look at it, I continued on my way. The sound of my phone ringing profusely, made me snatch it out of my pocket. The number that popped up wasn't saved in my phone, but I knew it belonged to the police department, so I rushed to answer it.

"Yeah?" I yelled through the phone.

"Hello…"

"Raven? Is that you?"

"Yeah, I need you to come get me."

"Come get you? What the fuck you doing at the jail?"

"It's a long story, but please hurry. I already called Taylor, but she didn't answer. Please call her and let her know what's going on."

Taking in everything she had to say, I rummaged through my car to find a pen and some paper, so I could write Taylor's number down. I couldn't figure out why the hell Raven had been arrested. As far as I knew, she was on her grown woman shit, lately. Her not telling me what it was over the phone let me know it was something serious. No matter what it was, I would go get my baby and show her I could be there for her like she had always been there for me.

Chapter Seven:
Taylor

Chaz and I were cuddled up at his crib, enjoying our time together. I felt like such a fool for leaving him to try to work things out with Sincere. He wasn't worth a penny as a man, so I knew he wouldn't be worth shit as a husband. That all went back to me not wanting to be a failure, but trust me, I've learned my lesson the hard way. Sometimes people had to really bump their head to know what they really needed in their life.

The sound of my phone ringing damn near scared the hell out of me. There was no reason for anyone to call me that late, so I ignored the call. The only person I could think of that could've been calling anyway, was Sincere, and I wasn't about to ruin the good time I was having with Chaz to deal with his bullshit.

"So, you not gonna answer the phone?" Chaz asked as my phone rung off the hook.

"No, it's probably Sincere and I don't want to ruin our night."

"Trust me, ma. There ain't shit that can ruin our night. Go ahead and answer it, I'ma go take a leak." Chaz informed me as he stood from the bed and made his way toward the bathroom.

By the time I got to my phone, it'd stopped ringing. Checking my call log, the number was one that I didn't recognize, so I was glad I didn't answer. Yes, I'm that typical person that won't answer the phone if I don't know the number. Sitting the phone back down, I started walking back toward the bed, until the phone rang again. I stormed back toward it, frustrated that someone was interrupting my evening.

Realizing it was a different number calling, I decided to go ahead and answer. Whomever it was, was desperately trying to reach me.

"What?" I rudely spoke, hoping it would cause whomever it was to hang up.

"Hey Taylor, it's Keon."

"Keon, who?"

"Raven's boyfriend." I rolled my eyes at the mere thought of him. After the shit Sincere disclosed at the club, if Raven stayed with him, she needed her ass beat. But, I guess that could be said about my ass as well for staying with Sincere all these years.

"What do you want Keon?"

"Raven's been trying to call you, she's been arrested."

When the words left his mouth, I immediately thought she'd been arrested for beating the shit out of him. Seriously, he couldn't be one of those punk ass niggas that ran to the police because their woman had gotten the upper hand on them.

"Which jail is she at?" I asked while I threw my clothes on.

Taking in everything he was telling me, I stepped inside the bathroom to let Chaz know what was going on. He told me to give him a few minutes to finish showering and he would ride with me. Ending the call, I searched the room for Chaz's phone. I needed to let Levi know what was going on with Raven. He would be upset if I didn't because it was evident he had feelings for her. She needed a man like Levi in her life instead of that sucka ass Keon.

Locating his phone, I typed in his code. I could vividly remember him putting it in several times. Once the phone was unlocked, I went to the call log in search of Levi's number, but something else caught my eye. There was a contact in his phone listed as *Devyn (BM)*. Surely, that couldn't be the same Devyn I shot earlier.

"What are you doing going through my phone?" Chaz stepped out of the bathroom with a towel wrapped around his waist.

"I was trying to get Levi's number, so I could let him know what was going on with Raven. I'm sure he would want to know."

"Well, it didn't look like you were making a call to me. It looked like you were checking to see if I had another woman's number in my phone or something."

He made his way towards me never taking his eyes off me.

Standing in front of me, Chaz snatched his phone out of my hand. When he looked down at it, I'm sure he noticed I'd clicked on Devyn's name. My plan was to call her to find out if she was the same woman Sincere had been fuckin' with. However, I couldn't get her number out of his phone in time enough to put it in mine. I had no choice but to go ahead and ask Chaz what I wanted to know.

"This Devyn person, is she the same one that works at the strip club?"

Chaz stood there and stared at me for a while, not saying a word, but he finally found the nerve to talk.

"Please tell me you're not the one who shot her." He skeptically stared into my eyes.

"It was an accident."

He moved away from me as if I were a stranger. That hurt my heart more than you could imagine.

"Why'd you shoot her? Maybe, somebody can tell me the real story." He inquired as he finally walked back toward me and reached for my hand.

"When I went back to be with Sincere, something seemed off about him. He told me that we were finally going to be able to work on having the baby I've always wanted. That was the only reason I decided to go back to him."

"Wait... Did you say your husband's name was Sincere?"

"Yeah. Why? You know him or something."

"I used to know someone by that name, but I'm sure it's not the same person. You remember the adoptive brother I told you about?"

"Yeah, what about him?"

"His name was Sincere. He moved away when he graduated high school and we never saw or heard from him again." Chaz confessed with a hint of dejection in his voice.

"Well, I'm sure this isn't the same guy because Sincere's parents are dead. Your adoptive parents are still living, right?"

"Yeah, they are. Now that we've determined this isn't the same person, continue with the story."

"Oh yeah, like I said, he told me he wanted to work on the baby I've always wan-." Chaz interrupted me again to ask a question of his own. One that somewhat agitated me, if I may add.

"So, all he had to do was mention a baby, and all was forgiven? That was fucked up, Taylor. Shit, I could've given you a baby if it meant you would've stayed." He was making a mockery out of my situation, and I didn't like it.

Surveying the room, I searched around for my keys. When I eyed them, I tried to brush past Chaz to get to them, but he wouldn't let me. He grabbed me by my wrist and pulled me back toward him.

"Chill out, Tay. I'm sorry. I'm still pissed off about the way things went down between us, but I'm not mad to the point that I would let you leave again. Now, tell me the rest of the story."

I thought about it long and hard before I decided to tell him anything else.

"If you can agree to not be a smartass, then I'll tell you, if not, then just let me leave." I chided, letting him know I meant business.

"That's fair enough, I'm sorry, baby," He conceded before he kissed me on my forehead.

"Sincere told me he had a meeting with a new client at a strip club. That sounded crazy as hell, but I let him think I believed him. I set things up with Raven to meet me at the club. When he left, I headed to the club right behind him. When I got there and we went inside, I walked in on that Devyn chick riding his dick. That nigga had the nerve to have his head thrown back like he was in pure bliss. I couldn't let that go down like that, so I reached for the gun Raven was carrying in her purse, closed my eyes, and pulled the trigger."

"So, you were trying to shoot Devyn?"

"Not at all. I was trying to shoot Sincere, but Devyn's dumb ass got in the way."

Chaz busted out laughing as if something was funny, but I found nothing about the situation to be funny.

"I'm sorry, but Devyn had me come get her from the hospital earlier. She told me some crazy woman came in and shot her for no reason, but now I'm hearing the truth from you, I can't help but laugh at how easily Devyn will try to play me for a fool."

"I'm sorry to put all of this on you and I'm sorry for shooting your baby's momma. That was one of those situations where she happened to be in the wrong place at the wrong time." I assured him. "Now, I have to go make sure Raven is good, we can talk about this some other time."

"There's nothing left to say about the situation. Devyn got what she deserved. She's going to get enough of sleeping with men that are already spoken for. I've warned her ass time and time again. Hopefully, she learned her lesson this time."

There were no other words spoken between the two of us as Chaz began to get dressed. It took him about five minutes, then we were headed out the door to the police station. Chaz opted to drive because he didn't think I could think straight since I was so worried about Raven and he was partially correct.

When we'd finally reached the police station, I hopped out the car without giving Chaz the opportunity to come to a complete stop. Running inside, I went straight up to the first desk I saw to see if I could find out anything about Raven. While I waited for her to get the officer working on Raven's case, Levi and Keon both came walking inside the lobby. Levi stopped to chat with Chaz for a minute while Keon walked straight toward me. Maybe, I was wrong for calling Levi when I knew Keon would be at the police station, but I didn't care.

"Did they tell you anything? Does she have a bail set? What's going on?" He fired off question after question before I was able to answer either one of them.

"They haven't told me anything, as of yet. She went to get someone who was familiar with the case and told me she would be right back. Calm down and wait." I informed him before I saw Levi and Chaz coming toward us.

"What the hell is going on, Taylor? Why is my girl being held here?" Levi finally came over to me and asked his own set of questions.

"I dunno anything yet, but hopefully we will know something soon."

I looked between both Levi and Keon. The expression on Keon's face let me know this shit wasn't about to end well at all, but that was his own fault. Keon had been doing his dirt for far too long. I'm sure he thought nobody else wanted Raven because of the way she acted at times, but he was about to see first-hand what people meant when they said one man's trash was another man's treasure.

Chapter Eight:
Sincere

When I arrived at the hospital, I was utterly disappointed that Taylor wasn't there. As my wife, she should've been the first face I saw when they rolled me inside. The only person I did see was Nyla's ass and even she was getting on my nerves.

"Somebody call my wife!" I rattled off as soon as I was placed insie of a room.

"Sir, your wife is already here." One of the nurses walked over to my bed to tend to me. "Would you like for me to send her in?" I nodded my head and waited for her to send Taylor inside.

I was pissed when I saw Nyla step inside the room instead of my real wife. She came toward me smiling and tried to give me a hug. I pushed her off me, letting her know her behavior was unacceptable.

"What the fuck are you doing in here?" I barked, causing the nurse to jump.

"Please keep it down, sir," The nurse informed me, trying to take control of the situation.

"You told me my wife was here. This bitch ain't my wife. Call her and find out where she is."

"No, don't call her. Taylor isn't coming. She made that plain and simple before she left the club."

Before I could respond to Nyla, the officer that responded to the call at the club came trolling inside the room.

"Excuse me, Mr. Griffith. May I have a moment of your time?"

"A moment of my time, for what? I've already told you what I had to say. Anything else you may want to discuss is irrelevant."

"I understand you're frustrated about this situation, but we're just trying to get to the bottom of things, and would really appreciate it if you would cooperate. Your cooperation will make this experience as smooth as it should be."

When the officer proceeded to ask questions, Nyla answered them, while I pondered over the entire situation. Karma was coming back and biting me in the ass for sure. I knew I fucked up majorly with Taylor, but she needed to understand that I was not going to let her go without a fight.

As I was deep in thought, an idea came to me on how I could get Taylor to reach out to me. The gun that was used to shoot me belonged to her best friend, Raven. Taylor loved Raven like a sister and would do anything to make sure Raven was good, so I was going to use that to my advantage. I decided to let the officer know what really happened at the club; well everything except for the part where Taylor shot Devyn.

"Raven shot me." I blurted out, creating silence in the room.

"What did you just say?" Nyla asked, confusingly.

"I said, Taylor's best friend, Raven, shot me. Her name is Raven Nickerson. She shot me because she was mad I kept cheating on Taylor."

"So, you mean to tell me your wife wasn't the one who shot you, it was her best friend? And you expect us to believe that?"

"You can believe whatever you want to believe, but I'm letting you know who did this. You can either arrest her or you can drop this case and stay the fuck out of my face."

Agitated that the officer was doubting me, I called myself trying to get out the bed so I could leave. When my foot touched the floor, I realized I never gave them the chance to look at my leg. I'm sure it wasn't anything major because they weren't in a hurry to make sure I was okay or to get the bullet out of me.

"Aaaaargghh..." I winced as the pain shot up my leg, through my body like an electric current.

"Mr. Griffith, we need you to stay still. The OR is completely full, so we have an on-call doctor coming in to take a look at your leg." The nurse talked, but I wasn't trying to hear anything she had to say.

The officer that was in my room finally left. I figured he was headed to pick Raven up. I hated to have to use Raven as a pawn in this game of Chess I played with Taylor. However, Raven would soon find out that she couldn't be friends with my wife and not be a casualty of war.

Any chance I got to use her, I would do it because she was the only way I would be able to get to Taylor. Finding out that I had Raven arrested would quickly get Taylor to try to work things out with me, just to get me to drop the charges.

"You need to stay your punk ass in that bed and let these folks look at you. I'm not trying to be a single parent because you couldn't follow directions and ended up bleeding to death." Nyla spoke up.

"I didn't ask you to come in here, and I'd really appreciate it if you took your dumb ass on. I already owe you an ass whipping for telling my wife about not only us, but the baby I wanted you to get rid of years ago."

"You couldn't make me do shit then, and you sure as hell can't make me do shit now." She boasted, loudly. "Oh, and since you want me to leave, I'll gladly do that, but know, I've been hiding my daughter for far too long. You claimed you were going to man up and be the father she needed you to be, but that didn't happen, and I'm sure it won't happen now. So, when you get those court papers stating you're ordered to pay child support, I don't want to hear shit else from you." That was the last thing she said before she tried to exit the room.

My whole world had been turned upside down in one night. If I would've known things would play out the way that they did, then I would've taken the risk of Devyn running to Taylor and telling her everything. At least then, I wouldn't have been shot, nor would I have been left wondering where she was, what she was doing, and who she was doing it with.

"Nyla, wait…" I had no choice, but to stop her.

If I would've allowed her to leave, then I wouldn't have had anyone there for me, so I needed her to stay. Besides, she was going to have to give me a ride home when it was all said and done.

"Wait for what? You've made it clear there isn't anything left here for us, so why should I sit around and listen to you ask for the next bitch." She said what she had to say, then left. I couldn't chase after her, nor could I stop her.

With Nyla not dealing with me any longer and Taylor nowhere to be found, I didn't know what to do. I knew the situation I was in was fucked up and I wouldn't wish it on my worst enemy. I had no choice but to think about how I was going to bounce back from this shit; that's if I was able to bounce back. Taylor wasn't going to make things easy for me, and Nyla let me know she was done, so what was a nigga to do?

"Is there anyone else you would like for us to call?" The nurse asked as if she was concerned.

"Yeah, I'm going to give you my real wife's number. I need you to call and act like I'm in a life or death situation and she needs to get down here."

"But it's not life or death, and I'm not about to lose my job fooling with you." She stated, sounding somewhat convincing, but I knew exactly what it would take to get her to change her mind.

Pulling my wallet out of my back pocket, I peeled off five one-hundred-dollar bills and laid them next to me on the stretcher. She hesitated for a moment but eventually came to retrieve it. I knew all too well, money talked and bullshit walked, so after she took the money, I patiently waited for Taylor to show up and be by my side the way she should've been from the beginning.

Chapter Nine:
Devyn

It had been days since I last saw my baby. I knew it was because Chaz was on that bullshit. He always kept Cassie away from me when he was pissed at me, but since he wanted to be a smart ass, I made plans to get up today and pop up at his house.

My shoulder was killing me, but I knew I would be fine. I couldn't keep lying around the house the way I'd been doing. Plus, I needed to make an appointment to get rid of this baby. Keon was furious with me, so I definitely didn't want the baby. I had no choice but to abort it. I'd already taken care of my hygiene, cleaned up my wound, and got dressed. Now, all I needed to do was comb my wild ass hair. I didn't have any cash to get my hair done, so I would rock a ponytail for a couple of days.

Once the pain stopped, I'd be back to my old self, and on a money chase. This time, I fucked up real bad, so I had no sponsors and my baby daddy wasn't fuckin' with me, so I was in a bad place. A thought popped in my head, so I figured I might've had a plan to come up with a little cash. I immediately pulled my phone out and shot Sincere a text.

Me: We need to talk.

Sincere: Bitch, I don't need to talk to you about anything.

Me: Listen, I just wanted you to know that I'm pregnant, you asshole.

Sincere: *Nah, that shit ain't mine, so you better move around with that bullshit.*

Me: *I'm sure it is, but I don't want it, so what you can do is give me the money to get rid of it.*

Sincere: *Look, Devyn, how do you even know this is my baby?*

Me: *Sincere, I don't want to argue with you about this. You can give me the money to get rid of it or we just wait until it gets here and your ass will be paying child support.*

After I sent the last text, I knew he wasn't gonna respond, so I decided to let the shit marinate on his brain. Now, I needed to hit Keon up with the same shit. I figured, I'd be able to get money from both of those assholes, that way, I'd have a couple of dollars in my pocket. I sat on the bed and thought over my plan a little more, then got up, so I could go to Chaz's house to see my baby.

Chaz always did that shit to me. I may not have been the mother of the year, but I still loved my daughter. I was getting angry all over again, just thinking about it, so I hurried out the door. All Chaz had to do was answer the fuckin' phone, then I wouldn't be doing this. Once I made it to my car, I started it, then pulled off.

Twenty minutes had passed before I pulled up, in front of Chaz's house. There were two cars parked out front, so I knew his ass had company, but I didn't care. I just hoped the bitch he had in there, stayed in her place.

What I said or did to Chaz about our child was between us and no other bitch.

Parking my car behind the one I didn't recognize, I exited and made my way toward the front door. Just when I was about to knock, the door flew open. If looks could kill, the bitch that opened the door would've been dead as hell.

"Chaz, you got company." The bitch that shot me had the nerve to grin in my face. Not thinking at all, I hauled off and slapped the bitch right in her face.

"You stupid ass hoe!" She yelled, then slapped me right back.

We started hitting each other, blow for blow, all in Chaz's doorway. Chaz must've been in our presence because I could hear his voice up close. The chick who shot me and I were fuckin' rockin'. It took Chaz a little minute to break us a part.

"What the fuck are y'all doing? My nosey ass neighbors all in the doorway watching this shit."

"That bitch hit me."

"Well, that's payback for shooting me you, stupid bitch. If I knew you were here, I would've came prepared to kill your dumb ass. What the fuck is she doing here anyway, Chaz?"

"Don't worry about why I'm here bitch. As a matter of fact, we're trading places. I got your man, and you can have mine."

Even though Chaz wasn't my man, I was still furious. I wanted to shoot that bitch; I swear I did.

"Would both of y'all shut the hell up and go the fuck in the house, now? Taylor, go sit over there on the chair, and Devyn, sit your ass on the couch. And y'all better act like y'all got some damn sense, because if anything pops off in my house, I'm fuckin' both of y'all up. Look at your dumb ass sitting over there in pain because you wanted to fight and shit." Chaz angrily spat at me, hurting my feelings a little by the way he was handling me in front of his new bitch.

"I didn't come over here to fight. I came over to see why you haven't been answering my calls and texts messages. I wanna see my daughter, Chaz. Every time we get into it or you're mad at me, you keep her away, and that's not fair. I'm her mother and I deserve to see her just as much as you do."

"I hear what you're saying, but you need to get your life in order, Devyn. I heard the story about what really went down at the club. Why didn't you just tell me the truth when I asked?"

"First of all, how do you know if anything you heard was true. You didn't bother to ask me one time to give you the real story, even though I was there and a part of the mess. But, that's not what I came over here to talk about. I know I need to get my shit together, Chaz, but when Cassie is with me, I don't be doing shit, but spending time with her. I never have a whole bunch of men around her the way that you think I do. Yeah, you found shit in my bathroom that belonged to a dude, but I never let Keon come over unless Cassie was sleep."

Fuck, I didn't mean to say Keon's name, I thought, but it was too late.

"Did you just say, Keon?"

"Yes, I did."

At that point, there was no reason for me to lie.

"Keon and I have been dealing with each other for a minute. And no, I didn't know he was Raven's man, just like I didn't know the other man was still with his wife. He told me he was leaving her and Keon promised me he was leaving his girl. I had no idea he never did. I'm sorry about all of this shit, Chaz. All I want to do is see my daughter."

"I'll bring her over after I go check on a couple things, but she's not staying the night with you until you get your shit together."

I wanted to oppose, but I figured I'd better take it or leave it.

"What did you tell me to come here for, Chaz?" Taylor interrupted him.

"Taylor, I wasn't done talking yet, so just chill. If me and you gone be kicking it, y'all two gone have to learn how to keep it cordial. I'm not saying y'all have to like each other or speak, but y'all will not be fuckin' fighting like kids when y'all come in contact with each other. What if my fuckin' daughter was here? I'ma tell y'all what would've happened, I would've beat the shit out of both of you.

Now, Taylor, if you want to go, you can, and Devyn, I'll bring Cassie over in a couple of hours."

I was fine with that, so I got up and headed out the door. The pain had started to come back and I was running out of Percs. I needed some more, so bad, but I didn't have a clue where to go. So many people in the hood knew Chaz and Keon, so that would be the talk of the town if they caught me buying Percs. With so many thoughts running through my mind while I drove home, I remembered something from working at the strip club. If any of the girls needed something to get high or whatever, Mace would look out for them. I quickly picked my phone up and sent Mace a text, asking if we could meet up real quick. When he replied *yes*, I knew I needed to hurry because Chaz was bringing Cassie over. I busted a U-turn in the middle of the street and headed to the club. I needed to get my fix before Chaz showed up with my little princess.

Chapter Ten:
Chaz

I couldn't believe those two were fighting in front of my house like they were two teenage girls. I could expect some shit like that from Devyn, but not Taylor. After I went off on them and kicked them out my house, I kind of got mad at myself for being mad at Taylor. I guess she had to defend herself and I couldn't blame her because I would've done the same thing. The thought that kept running through my mind was, *what if Cassie were home?* That's why I had to sit them down and let them know the deal.

Clearing my head, I headed out to go run a few errands. I ran by the bar to make sure shit was running smoothly and did a couple of other things before I went to pick up Pop's medicine. Afterward, I headed to my parent's house to drop off the medicine, and pick up Cassie, so I could take her to go see Devyn. Once I made it to their house, I parked my car, then headed on the inside like I lived there. Smelling something coming from the kitchen, I knew that's where Mama had to be, so I went straight in there to see her.

"Hey, Mama, what you cookin' up in here, it smells good?"

"My baby and I are baking some cookies."

"Well, I'm right on time, then. Can I eat some with y'all?"

"Yayyyyyyy daddy!" Cassie yelled, excitedly, causing Mama D and me to laugh.

"Where Pop at, Mama?"

"Chile, he's upstairs watching TV."

"Okay, I'm going to go check him out. Call me when the cookies are finished."

I left my two favorite ladies in the kitchen and headed upstairs to check on Pops. Standing outside of their room, I knocked on the door and waited for him to tell me to come in.

"Hey, old man, what you got goin' on in here?"

"Ain't shit goin' on in here. What you been up to, and how's business been going for you?"

I watched him as he spoke, and realized he looked a lot better since he'd been taking his medicine and eating right.

"Business is fine, but that's not what's been stressing me out lately."

"What's goin' on, Son? Talk to me."

"Well, I met this chick named Taylor. I've been dealing with her for a while, but she's married. She and her husband are going through it right now, so we've been hanging real tight."

"So, what's the problem?"

"The problem is that we hung tight for a while when I first met her, but she all of a sudden upped and left me, saying she was going to make it work with him. I figured we were done at that point until a couple of days ago, when she came prancing into the bar, crying her eyes out because she'd just shot some chick that she caught riding her husband at the damn strip club."

"Well, damn, Son, this sounds like a damn BET movie."

"That ain't even the worse part, Pops. How bout the stripper that she shot was Devyn's ass."

"Get the fuck out of here, Son, you got to be kiddin' me."

"Naw, and guess who popped up at my house today while Taylor was there."

"Not Devyn's ass."

"Yes, Devyn and Taylor just so happened to answer the door. They started arguing and Devyn just up and slapped Taylor's ass. Of course, Taylor slapped her ass back, then they started rockin' in my front door where the damn neighbors could see the shit. I made them both stop and sit on the couch, so I could tell them how I was feeling before I kicked them both out."

"Damn, Son, you have a lot going on. How do you plan on handling this?"

"Well, I told Devyn she needed to get her shit together if she ever wanted Cassie to stay over her house again. Until she does, all she'll be getting is supervised visits. Now with Taylor, I don't know what to do, Pops, because I'm really feeling her, but at the same time, I'm scared she might wanna run back to her husband again."

"I can't tell you that you don't need to start anything with her until she gets a divorce because you're already involved with her. The feelings are clearly there. What you need to do is be careful, Son. That's the only advice I can give you. After the last incident, she might be fed up and done with her husband for good this time.

"I hope so, Pops, because she got me feeling some type of way, and I don't usually get like this over no females."

"It sounds to me like she put it on you." Pops teased while chuckling.

"Come on now, old man, stop talking about stuff you don't know about."

"Shit, I know all about it, that's why I've been married for over forty years. You talking to a vet, Son. Your mama stole my heart years ago, and she's been all I've ever wanted since then. Once you get the love of your life, you ain't gone give a damn about being whipped. Hell, half my friends that teased me about being in love ain't ever got married and they still some lonely ole bastards."

Those talks were what I lived for. I loved when me and Pops sat and kicked it. He didn't kick anything to me, but knowledge. It also made me think that maybe Taylor and I did need to chill until she figured out what she wanted to do about her husband. It would be hard to stay away from her, but I believed it would be a good move.

"I hear you, Pop. To be honest, what you and Mama got, is something I'm looking forward to real soon."

"You'll get it one day soon, Son. You're a good man with good intentions, so when you find that special lady, take good care of her and give her the world. If shit goes all wrong with Ms. Taylor, don't worry yourself about it; if it's meant to be, it'll work itself out and y'all will find your way back to each other."

"Alright, Pops, thanks for the conversation. I really needed to hear that. Now, let me get down there and eat some cookies with Mama and Cassie. Oh, yeah, I picked up your medicine. It's downstairs."

"Okay, Son, thank you so much. I really appreciate you for all you do for yo Mama and me. You became successful and didn't turn your back on us, and that means the world to us."

"No thanks needed, Pops. If it wasn't for you and mama taking me in, it ain't no telling where I'd be, and for that, I owe you both my life." I walked over to my pop and gave him a hug before I left the room.

"Okay, enough of that soft ass shit. Hugging me like I'm Taylor and shit." Pops hollered as I walked away.

After goin' back downstairs and eating a couple of cookies, I bussed it up with Mama for a minute, then headed out, so I could take Cassie to see Devyn for a couple hours. I kissed my mom and gathered Cassie's things. We said our goodbyes before we exited the house.

As I walked out the door with Cassie in my arms, she yawned. I kind of felt bad because it was her time to visit her mom and she was tired. I strapped my baby in her seat and kissed her forehead before I went around to the driver's side of the car and got in. It wasn't long before I started the car and we were on our way.

It took about a half hour to get to Devyn's house from where my parents lived. Cassie was knocked out in the backseat for the duration of the ride. When I pulled up to Devyn's house, I parked my car and hopped out to grab Cassie, so I could carry her inside the house. I knocked on the door three times, but Devyn wasn't answering. That shit pissed me off because she knew I was coming.

Still holding my keys in my hand, I decided to just use my key to get in. Once I got the door open, I headed to the living room and laid Cassie on the couch while I went to find Devyn. I looked into the kitchen and saw she wasn't there, so I headed to her bedroom. When I made it to her room, I saw her lying on the bed like she was in a deep sleep. I called her name and didn't get a response, so I walked to where she was. I called her name as I took each step, and was shocked she didn't answer me or move. Finally reaching the bed, I realized that she was lying in blood.

"Devyn, what the fuck, man?" I yelled as I pulled my phone out of my pocket.

I called Devyn's name and shook her, and it freaked me out because she still didn't move. Urgently, I called 9-1-1 to get help. I would've just taken her to the hospital myself, but I didn't want to move her.

"9-1-1, what's your emergency?" The dispatcher asked once she got on the phone.

"Hello, I need an ambulance as soon as possible. I found my daughter's mother lying in blood."

"Ok, sir, calm down, and tell me where the blood is coming from." I looked at Devyn closely and noticed the blood was coming from between her legs.

"It looks like she's bleeding between her legs."

"Ok, sir, check her pulse for me."

"She has a pulse, but it's faint."

"What's the address?" She began asking me all kinds of questions, which irritated me. I gave her the address and Devyn's name; anything else they needed, they would have to get once the ambulance arrived.

"Alright, the paramedics should be out front of your house shortly, sir. Is she pregnant?"

"No, not that I'm aware of, but what the fuck does that have to do with anything?"

"From what you were describing, it sounds as though she could be having a miscarriage, and she probably passed out from losing too much blood."

I was in total disbelief at the thought of Devyn having a miscarriage. If indeed that's what that was. I didn't even know her ass was pregnant.

There was a sudden knock at the door, and I knew it was the paramedics, so I ran to open it. After I let them inside the house, I went and picked Cassie up and strapped her in her car seat. I stood and waited by the car for the paramedics to roll Devyn out, so I could let them know I would meet them at the hospital. It didn't take long for them to come walking outside with Devyn hooked up to oxygen and everything.

"Is she going to be okay?" I rushed toward them to ask.

I was honestly concerned. Devyn and I may have had our differences, but I would never want anything bad to happen to her.

"She'll be just fine, we just need to get her to the hospital, so the doctors can take care of her. What hospital do you want us to take her too, sir?"

"Cooper is fine since it's the closest. I'll be there in a little while. I have to drop my daughter off at my parent's house."

"Okay, that's fine. Can you tell me her name again, sir?"

"Her name is Devyn Smith." I gave them as much information about Devyn as I could remember.

"Alright, when you get there, just give her name to the person at the front desk and they'll tell you everything you need to know."

After the paramedic told me that, I hopped in my car and headed straight to my parent's house. I was going so fast, I prayed the whole way there, that I didn't get pulled over.

Chapter Eleven:
Raven

When I arrived at the police station and heard what the charges were, I instantly grew sick to my stomach. I knew Sincere was only doing that shit out of spite. He could care less that I shot his ass. It was the fact that I was close to Raven that drove him to reach out to the police. But, if he thought having me arrested was going to earn him a spot back in her life, then he was a lie.

After questioning me about the situation and with Nyla and Sincere's information not matching up, the police had no choice, but to let me go. They did warn me not to leave town until the investigation was complete, and I was perfectly fine with that.

Thanks to Taylor and Levi, I didn't have to spend the night in jail. The shit was embarrassing as hell that I was even put in that situation. I couldn't believe Sincere was bogus enough to do some shit like that to me; then again, yes, I could.

I was shocked when I walked out to find Levi, Taylor, Chaz, and Keon's ass, standing out in the waiting area, waiting for them to release me. The way Levi and Keon looked at each other was crazy and I didn't understand why, when neither one of them was my man. Levi being there did peak my interest, though. The fact that he didn't know shit about me, but still came there to rescue me, spoke volumes. But, I didn't know why Keon's dumb, broke ass even came. It wasn't like his ass had the money to get me the fuck out. I can't even believe I fucked with a loser like his ass. Hell, the only reason I even called him was because I wanted him to call Taylor since she wasn't answering the phone for me.

"Thank ya'll." I went around hugging Chaz, Taylor and Levi.

"So, you just gonna act like you don't see me standing here?"

"I'm not acting like shit. I see you, but I don't feel the need to acknowledge you."

"Aye, I'm not gonna let you keep talking to me like I ain't shit."

"Hell, you ain't." I blasted back annoyed with the way he was acting. His ass could've at least waited until we stepped out of the police station before he started acting stupid.

"Don't make me fuck you up Raven."

"Back down lil nigga." Levi stepped in front of me to address Keon. "I don't know what you've done to her in the past and I honestly don't care, but if you think you're gonna do something to her, then you better guess again." The look in Keon's eyes worried me.

Keon opted not to say anything else to me or anyone standing around me. He quickly made his way out the front door, but something told me that I hadn't seen the last of him.

"What's up, ma, what you over there thinking about?" Levi asked as he walked toward me, snapping me out of my thoughts.

Levi had been staying at my house with me since I got my ass out of jail that night. All he'd done was go to work and come back here to be with me. I knew I said I wasn't gon' deal with anyone so soon, but it was something about him that made me want to explore this shit more. I hadn't given the cookie up, just yet, but I knew the time was coming.

"Nothing, I was just thinking about what went down with me shooting Sincere's ass over him telling me about Keon's dog ass."

"Don't worry about that, baby. You were just in your feelings."

"I shouldn't have let those two assholes take me there. Now, what if we go to court, and I get convicted for the shit and have to do time?"

"You ain't doing no time and that nigga gon' drop those charges. Don't even worry about it, Chaz and I have it covered."

I didn't know what the hell they had going on, but I was gon' let them do them.

"Levi, can I ask you something and you be honest with me?"

"Yup, you can ask me anything, beautiful."

"Why are you doing all this for me? You barely even know me."

"I ain't even gon' lie, but when I first saw you, I was clowning you to Chaz, but after I sat and talked to you, that shit changed everything. Now, here I am, trying to get to know you and you playing hard to get. You act like you don't know what it feels like to let a real nigga love on you.

"Levi, gone somewhere kicking all that game. Dude's stay talking that real nigga shit and when the time comes, they be on some fuck nigga shit. I'm sick of getting hurt and giving my heart to muthafuckas that don't deserve it."

"Well, as soon as you're ready, I'ma show you what real niggas do. Now, what are we getting into tonight? Do you wanna stay in and I cook you something or do you wanna go out to eat?"

"I really don't feel like goin' out, so we can just order out and watch movies all night."

"Oh, so you want the kid to spend the night again?" Levi teased with a cheesy ass grin on his face.

"I guess you can stay again, it ain't like I'm doing shit else."

"Don't say it like that, big head," Levi said while still smiling.

"So, tell me, Mr. Levi, why a fine ass brother like you don't have a wife and any kids."

"I don't have any kids because I haven't met anyone worthy enough to birth my children. And I'm not married, yet, because I wasn't ready. Marriage is something that should be done when two people are ready. I'm one of those types of men that once you marry me, it's forever. So, until I meet someone that's ready and we in love, that's who will be the mother of my children." He spoke with so much sincerity in his voice.

"I heard that! I've been in so many messed up relationships I don't know what to expect these days. Then, seeing what Taylor went through in her marriage always made me look at the idea of marriage differently."

"You can't go off what you see someone else going through because not every man is a fuckboy like Taylor's husband."

"You're right, but I also haven't met any niggas that were different, so I guess any future relationship I get into, that person is gon' have to show me it's more to life than fuckin' bum ass niggas. And to be honest, these niggas got me ready to see what dating a bitch is all about."

"Raven, shut yo crazy ass up. You ain't trying no bitches out," Levi asserted while chuckling.

"I'm just joking, bitches are probably just as bad."

While Levi and I talked, thoughts of how I handled Keon when he came over popped into my head, causing me to laugh.

"What you laughing at, crazy girl?"

"I was just thinking about how Keon came over that night after all that shit went down at the club."

'What he do?"

"That nigga came in here like he didn't have a care in the world. I was sitting in the dark with tears in my eyes and my gun in my hand. Once he turned the light on and saw me sitting there with the gun pointed at him, the look on his face was priceless. He didn't know what was going on," I offered while still cracking up.

"What would you know about guns, shorty?"

"You'd be surprised at what I know about guns. My daddy taught me everything I needed to know when he was in the streets."

"What's your pops name, so I can see if I know him?"

"His name is Rasul Nickerson and he used to be heavy in these streets. My parents didn't have the best jobs, but they were great parents to me growing up. They taught me how to be both book and street smart."

'That's what's up... Beauty, brains, and can buss her guns when need be. I think I'm in love already."

"Boy, be quiet. You ain't in no love, yet." I shook my head and laughed at Levi.

"But, on the real, I heard of your pops. He's a street legend. He still gets talked about a lot. How's he doing these days?"

"He's great. He and my mom are still together."

"That's what's up, so finish telling me what else happened with Keon."

"Of course, you know he tried to talk to me, but I wasn't beat. I cut him off and told him he had a certain amount of time to get his shit and get out. Once he figured out I wasn't playing with his lame ass, he hurried to get two little trash bags worth of his shit and went flying out my front door."

"Girl, you sound like you can be hell in a relationship."

"I'm a good woman. I cook, clean, wash clothes, and still work a regular nine to five, so when I'm putting my all in this and you fuck over me, you need to be very careful because I will kill you. My daddy told me how to get in touch with the cleanup crew and I got the number on speed dial, so trust me when I say, I don't play no games."

"I hear you over there, killa. Remind me not to get on your bad side."

"Something tells me that you're a lot different from the rest, Levi, so I'm sure I don't have to worry about that."

"You're right, Ma. I'm cut from a different cloth and believe me when I tell you, they don't make them like me no more," Levi jested, cockily.

Levi and I spent the rest of the night talking and watching movies. The time I spent with him, I really enjoyed. I was happy we clicked how we did and couldn't wait to see where things went with us.

Chapter Twelve:
Taylor

Chaz was out of his muthafuckin' mind, thinking I was going to let that bitch he had for a baby momma put her damn hands on me and I not do anything in return. It wasn't that type of party. He had me so fucked up, it was a shame. The only thing I could do was go home because I didn't want to be around him.

Sincere was the last muthafucka I wanted to see, as well, but I needed to get some of my shit out of that house and get ghost on his ass. I hoped like hell they kept his low down ass at the hospital, so he wouldn't be all in my damn face, trying to talk and shit. Talking was something we shoulda did years ago, before he decided to stick his dick off in the next bitch.

Pulling into my driveway, I was relieved when I didn't see Sincere's car. The hospital had been blowing me up, so I knew they thought I would come get his ass. *A muthafuckin' lie*, I thought to myself. That nigga was getting no more of my precious time with his worthless ass. I shoulda shot him in the dick. I bet none of those hoes would've wanted his ass, then.

While I sat in my car thinking about the crazy shit that had gone down the past two days, Chaz crossed my mind. I wanted to know why he didn't let me beat his bitch down. He knew she was in the wrong, so I had every right to beat the shit out of her. She'd get enough of fuckin' with other people's men. I hope she catches something and they have to sew her damn pussy shut.

Deciding to call Chaz, I quickly pulled out my phone and dialed his number before I stepped out of my car.

"Taylor, now is really not a good time."

"Why? You around that bitch ass baby momma of yours?"

"Taylor, please let me call you back."

"No, you're about to hear what the fuck I have to say."

Maybe, I was being too harsh with Chaz, but I was fed up with men as a whole. In the short period of time I've known Chaz, he'd done something to me. He'd made me feel shit my own husband hadn't been able to make me feel in years. I wasn't sure I was ready to let any of those feelings go, but at the same time, I wasn't about to let him play me to the left for that bitch, Devyn. She didn't deserve to have kids with a man like him. That should've been my daughter. I'm around Cassie more than Devyn is anyways.

"Taylor, are you there?"

Hearing Chaz speak reminded me that he was on the phone.

"Why wouldn't I be? Are you ready to listen?"

"Hold on, let me step away from everybody."

Once Chaz said that, I wondered if that nigga was having a party or some shit. What reason did his ass have for being around other people? After that fight went down, he should've had his ass somewhere sulking and thinking about the way he put me out when all I was trying to do was defend myself. That was some fucked up shit if you asked me. But you not asking me, right? Well whatever, I'm telling y'all asses that it was fucked up.

Seriously, who the hell did he think was going to stand there and allow someone to hit on them and they not do anything to tag they asses back? I mean, shit, don't let the pretty face fool you. I'm beautiful and classy, but that shit turns on and off like windshield wipers. Fuck he thawt.

"Okay, go ahead and talk."

"Where are you?"

"None of that matters right now. Apparently, you feeling froggy, and got some shit you want to get off your chest, so go for it."

Not liking the way he was talking to me, I began to think long and hard about how I should approach the topic. I had every intention of going the hell off on his ass for the way he handled things, but I was starting to think he wasn't going to let me. See, Sincere would let me have my moment of cussing and would just drown my ass out. For some reason, I felt the minute I went at Chaz the wrong way, he would hand my ass right back to me.

"Talk, Tay, I ain't got all day. I told you now wasn't a good time, but since you insist on bossin' up on a nigga, say what you gotta say. But, watch how the fuck you say it because I'ma give your ass more than you bargained for.

I'm a whole different breed than that weak shit you probably get from your husband. So, you've been warned."

"What happened? All I want to know is, what happened? Why'd you make me leave when I wasn't in the wrong?"

"I tried to get y'all to stop, Tay. I live in a good neighborhood. I'm trying to raise my daughter a certain kind of way. You think I need people picking on her because two women were acting ratchet around her father?"

"I understand that, but she started it. If anything, you should've made her leave. Not me, I feel like you were choosing her over me. It's like you were allowing her to get away with something by putting me out, too. That's exactly what she wanted and you gave it to her on a silver platter."

"You can think that shit if you want to, Tay, but I can assure you that wasn't it at all. I'm really feeling you, ma, but I expect my women to act a certain way. I have a reputation to maintain. You should understand that. What if I was in front of your house and fought your husband?"

"I wouldn't give a damn as long as you beat his muthafuckin' ass," I told him, honestly.

The way I was feeling, he could tie Sincere's ass to the back of his car and drag his ass. I promise I wouldn't give two fucks about what happened to that nigga. At that point, he deserved any and everything that happened to him.

"Fighting isn't the answer, Taylor. You and I both know that. Maybe, I was wrong for the way I handled things, then."

"All I'm saying is, if a nigga walked right up to you and slapped the fuck out of you, you gonna let them walk away without doing anything to them?"

"This ain't about me. This was about you and Devyn."

"Answer the question, Chaz."

"I'm not answering that."

His refusal to answer the question let me know he would put a nigga on his ass quick if he raised up on him for no reason. I wasn't a fool by any means.

"Exactly, that's what I thought. Your ass would try to bury a nigga."

"Men and women are different and you know that." He called himself trying to justify his answer.

"Fuck all that, you know ain't nobody in their right mind gonna let somebody run up on them and they not do shit unless they scared. It's cool, though. You made ya decision, and once again, it was the wrong decision. Things don't seem to ever work out for us."

"Don't say that, Ta-."

As Chaz talked, I went ahead and ended the call. There was nothing left for us to discuss.

When I told him that he had made the wrong decision, I meant that shit. He pretty much let me know he was rocking with Devyn, which was cool with me, considering they have more history. Besides, she gave him something that I probably could never give him; a baby!

Cutting my car off, I decided to go ahead and go in the house. I wanted to get as much of my shit as I could before Sincere brought his duck lip ass back to the house. I'd had enough of his shit to last a lifetime. There was no way I could handle any more of his shit; especially not today.

Begrudgingly making my way inside the house, I could hear music playing in Sincere's office. I wanted to shoot myself for not thinking to check the garage. That only meant his punk ass had hidden his car in the garage so he could catch me slipping. Since I was already there, I wasn't about to go back out the door without the stuff I showed up to get. Just call me cat woman, because I was about to tiptoe around this bitch like a cat, hoping I could be in and out before he even realized I was there.

Chapter Thirteen:
Sincere

Devyn had some damn nerve texting me, talking about her ass was pregnant. I knew damn well it wasn't mine because I hadn't been fuckin' with her long enough for her to think she was pregnant.

There I was sitting in my office at home, waiting to see if Taylor would show up. She was so mad at me that her ass wouldn't return any of my calls or texts. I knew her ass wouldn't be gone too long because all her clothes and favorite things were here.

I sat in my office, listening to old school R&B, and allowed my mind to drift away with the smooth sounds of Luther Vandross. It would only be a matter of time before Taylor came home, and I was more than prepared for her ass. Whatever needed to be done, I would do to get her to hear me out.

The music was loud enough for me to comfortably groove to it, but not loud enough to stop me from hearing Taylor when she pulled up. I peeped out the blinds and saw her in her car having a heated discussion with someone. I'm sure it wasn't nobody but Raven's bitch ass.

Knowing her, she was probably mad that I allowed Raven to be arrested. I didn't give a damn about that, though. Had she been the wife she was supposed to be and been at the hospital to check on me and cater to my needs, none of that shit would've happened. Hell, I had to depend on Nyla to get me home, which was fucked up because I never allowed anyone to catch me slipping and find out where I laid my head. That would give them grounds to bring bullshit to my house and that was something I didn't tolerate. Don't bring stupid shit to my doorstep and don't walk around thinking it's cool to disrespect my wife.

I heard Taylor walk through the door, and I knew she thought I wasn't home, but I'm sure the music playing was a dead giveaway that I was here. Not hearing her walking, let me know that her ass was trying to tip around and do what she wanted to do in order to avoid me. I allowed her enough time to think I didn't know she was here until I popped out to show her otherwise. It was a struggle for me to get to the room, considering I was shot in the leg and had to rely on crutches to get around; something I wasn't used to.

Stepping inside the room, I witnessed Taylor throwing whatever she could, inside of a suitcase. When she laid eyes on me, she began to speed up her pace. She didn't even bother to acknowledge I was in the room which really started to make my blood boil. How the hell are you gonna come to a place where I pay the majority of the bills and disrespect me like I'm not there?

"I know you see me standing here, Tay. We need to talk."

"Naw, we needed to talk before you started passing your dick around." She quickly rebutted.

"Touché."

I knew I deserved that, so there was no need for me to argue with her.

"You're right. There's nothing I can do to change that, but I want to know what I can do to make things right between us again?"

"You can start by dropping dead."

Her sarcasm made the palms of my hand itch. The thought of slapping her ass across the bed crossed my mind, but I knew that would be something that we'd never bounce back from.

"Very funny, Taylor. I know you don't mean that shit," I retorted, moving closer to her.

"Do you see me laughing? I swear I don't see my face turning up to a smile or any damn thing else. And if your punk ass moves any closer to me, I'm going to cut your dick off and sit here and watch you bleed to death."

Somehow, her expression let me know her ass meant every word she said. Did I really push her to her breaking point? Damn, she shot at my ass and ended up hitting someone else. She allowed her best friend to shoot my ass in the leg, and she didn't even come to the hospital to see about a nigga. Now, she's threatening to chop my man off, knowing damn well how much she loved his ass.

"I'm sorry, Taylor."

"Damn right you're sorry. You're the sorriest muthafucka I've ever met in my life. I wish I never laid eyes on you. Hell, even then, I should've kept walking. All these years of my life wasted on somebody who was never worth it."

"Now listen, I'm not going to keep tolerating you talking to me out the side of your neck, so you better cut that shit out, right now. I told you I was sorry. I'm not about to sit here and kiss your ass or beg you to forgive me."

"That's good because I didn't ask your ass to."

Taylor continued with packing her things like I wasn't standing there. I told her I wasn't going to beg her, but I was out of options. I tried to get down on my knees like JoJo from Jodeci had done when he looked like a rat with all that crying and begging shit, but I couldn't. Then, I thought about doing that Keith Sweat kind of begging, but I figured she wouldn't go for that shit either. My only other option was to allow her time to herself. That was the only thing I could think of.

"Maybe, if you had time to yourself to think about things, you'll come to your senses. You'll realize what I did was out of selfishness, not with the intent to hurt you. I know we can make this shit right."

"Naw, what you need to be worrying about is how you can be a father to the child out there. You know, that's what bothers me the most about this whole situation."

I knew that shit was coming.

Taylor had asked for years for us to have a baby, but I kept telling her we weren't ready, even though we were more than ready. We were financially set, great in our careers, had houses and cars, and I knew she would make a great mother, but I just didn't want any kids. I didn't want to break her heart by telling her I didn't want to be a father period, so I kept the charade going. Meanwhile, I was playing somewhat of a daddy to a child I'd been hiding.

"You're right. I was wrong for that shit. I kept you from doing something you really wanted to do out of stupidity. You would've made a great mother. I took that chance from you, a while back, but I'm really ready to make it happen now."

"You can make it happen all you want, but I can assure you that you won't be making it happen with me."

Taylor closed her suitcase, then brushed past me, almost knocking me down in the process.

"Damn, bitch, you see I can barely move, so you gonna knock down a handicapped man. You ain't right, Tay."

"Naw, your mind ain't right and your dick ain't either. Damn shame, it took for me to get some outside dick for me to realize that what you had wasn't worth a damn."

There had to be a way that my ears were deceiving me. For a minute, I thought Taylor may have stepped out on me, but I crossed that thought out of my mind when I got her to start back acting right. However, she just up and admitted that she was fucking around on me and thought I would allow her to walk out the door without facing any consequences behind the shit; oh, hell nah.

"Get your ass back here, Taylor. What the fuck you just say?"

As fast as I walked with those crutches, you would've never guessed this was my first time using any.

"Stop moving, and get back here. You can't say no shit like that, then think you can just walk away."

"Watch me!" She asserted as she turned, and walked out the door.

The only thing I could do was take my time to get downstairs, so I wouldn't fall and hurt myself. I should've reached out and wrapped that fuckin' crutch around her damn neck, but I wasn't thinking straight. The shit she'd just revealed to me had me fucked up in the head. How could she step out on me? She was supposed to love, honor, obey, and cherish my black ass, but you see how the fuck she did me. Then, she walking around this bitch like everything all copasetic and shit. Let me find out she let that nigga nut in her, then allowed me to turn right back around and suck his nut out of her while I was eating her pussy. I will kill both their asses.

By the time I got down the stairs, Taylor was pulling out of the driveway. There was no way I would be able to catch up with her, so I allowed her to leave. What I did do, was pull out my phone and call my nigga Trey. I always relied on him when I needed to dig up dirt on people. I was going to get him to follow Taylor around and dig up as much shit on her and whomever she was cheating with as I could get. Then, I would turn around and use that shit against her in court. If she wanted to leave, she would pay for it by giving me alimony every month. Yep, I was going to say she abandoned my black ass.

See, while she was so wrapped up in the fact that I cheated on her, none of the bitches that I fucked with would go to court and testify against me. There was no way she would be able to prove any of my infidelities; especially if she can't produce the daughter that I shared with Nyla. However, if I had Trey to follow her and he caught her out in the open, creeping with the next nigga, then it was a wrap for her. All her money would be as good as mine, and I wouldn't feel bad about it.

Consider me to be Kendu Issacs and her ass to be Mary J. Blige. Even though I was in the wrong first, she would feel it more than me when I hit her where it would hurt her most; in her damn pockets.

Chapter Fourteen:
Devyn

I woke up in so much pain and didn't know where I was until I saw the IV in my arm. Looking around, I noticed Chaz sitting in a chair next to me. I didn't know what happened to me, but I knew the pain was excruciating.

"Chaz, wake up!" I yelled, causing him to jump out of his sleep, looking crazy.

"What's up, Devyn? You alright, ma?" Chaz questioned walking over to me; our eyes immediately connected.

"What happened to me?"

"You had a miscarriage, ma. You lost a lot of blood."

I knew I wasn't sure about what I wanted to do with the baby, but hearing I'd miscarried brought tears to my eyes.

"Oh, my, God!" I screamed while rubbing my stomach.

Chaz pulled me close to him and kissed my forehead.

"You gon' be just fine, Devyn. Stop crying, ma," he said while wiping away my tears.

"Chaz, what's wrong with me? Why am I the way that I am? I can't ever do shit right. All I want to do is to change my life and do right by Cassie." My words were genuine.

"Well, all you need to do from now on is do better, Devyn. Now, tell me this, did you know you were pregnant?"

I dreaded him asking me that question, but I knew I had to truthfully answer him.

"Yes, I did, but I didn't know what I was going to do about it," I informed him, honestly.

"Did you know who the father was?"

"Yes, it was Keon's baby, and he didn't want anything to do with it. That's why I was thinking about getting rid of it."

"Well, I'ma tell you now, you damn sure scared the shit out of me when I walked in and found you lying in a puddle of blood."

I just sat there and listened to him tell the story of how he found me.

"I'm so sorry, Chaz. Where was Cassie at?"

"She was sleep. I left her on the couch while I went to check on you. They said you had a high dosage of Percocet in your system which knocked your ass out. Why were you taking those pills like that, Devyn?"

"I was in so much pain today. Between the bullet wound, and the stomach cramps I was having, I needed something to take the pain away. I figured the stomach pain was nothing, so I just popped a couple of Percs and laid down. I remembered how my stomach used to cramp when it was stretching while I was pregnant with Cassie and that's what I thought was happening this time. I see now, those cramps meant I was miscarrying, which is something I never expected to happen."

"Devyn, you need to do better, ma. That's all I'ma keep saying to you until you do it. I'm sick of going through this with you."

"I know Chaz and I swear I'm gon' change for Cassie."

A knock at the door interrupted our conversation.

"Hello, Ms. Smith, I'm Dr. Louis. How are you feeling?"

"I'm okay, just in a little pain."

"Okay, a little pain is to be expected, but overall, everything is looking fine with you. Your vitals are back to normal, which is great. However, we still want you to stay overnight, so we can monitor your levels. Are you aware that you miscarried?"

"Yes, I'm aware. Is everything ok? Can you tell me why I lost the baby?"

"We think it's because of the stress that you've been under lately. To our understanding, you were recently shot, then you took a lot of pain pills that weren't good for you, but you're okay now and you'll be able to have more kids in the future. I'm going to need you to follow up with your OBGYN. Once you're released, please call and make an appointment."

"Alright, Dr. Louis, thanks so much."

"You're welcome, Ms. Smith. We'll be sending you home with pain meds and vitamins."

After the doctor informed me of everything I needed to know, he left out.

"Are you hungry? I'll go get you something to eat," Chaz asked.

"Yes, I'm hungry, but I want you to know that you don't have to stay here with me, Chaz if you have something else to do."

"Come on, Devyn. Don't start that shit again. I ain't goin' nowhere, but to get you something to eat, so we can chill for the rest of the night."

Chaz hopped up and headed out the door to get us something to eat. While he was gone, I sat and stared at the wall, wondering how the hell my life got this way. Chaz and I were once happy; he loved me and I fucked it all up. Now, he's finally seeing someone else, and my heart hurts. Yeah, I done messed around with plenty of niggas, but I ain't never gon' love anybody like I love my baby daddy.

The longer I sat up, the more the pain came back, so I pushed the button to call the nurse for some pain pills. Five minutes later, the nurse came strolling inside the room.

"Here's your pain pills, Ms. Smith."

"Thank you!"

"Would you like anything to eat or drink besides water?" The nurse probed.

"No, I have someone bringing me some food, thanks so much!"

"You're welcome. If you need anything else, feel free to hit the button again."

Once she'd left out, it didn't take long for the pills to take effect. I didn't know what the hell they gave me, but I knew it had me dozing off less than ten minutes after I'd taken it.

****

"Yo, Devyn, wake up." I heard Chaz call me.

"Hey, what took you so long?"

"Devyn, I wasn't even gone that long. They must've given your ass some pain meds. Wake up so you can eat." He paused, then started pulling the food out the bag. "I got you a cheese steak with fried onions, ketchup, mayo, and a peach tea."

"Thank you, baby daddy."

"You're welcome, now get ya ass up and eat."

I raised the bed up and fixed the table in front of me so I could eat.

"Tomorrow, when you take me home, can we stop by your parents' house so I can see Cassie?"

"Who said I was taking you home? Damn, you just want a nigga to do everything."

"You know what, Chaz, never mind, you don't have to do shit else for me."

"I'm just joking, Devyn, calm down. Of course, we can go see Cassie. You know what, we can just go pick her up and we can all spend the day together."

"Chaz, you really don't have to do that. I wouldn't wanna make your girlfriend mad."

"First of all, I don't have a girlfriend, we're just friends. Secondly, Cassie is ready to see you, so I know when she wakes up tomorrow, she is gon' wanna see us both."

"I'm sorry, I didn't mean to snap on you, Chaz."

"I know you didn't mean it."

Chaz stated as we both ate.

Chaz and I continued to watch TV and discuss future plans. Like always, when I told Chaz what I wanted to do, he told me he would help me as much as he could. We even talked about the situation with him and Taylor. He let me know he was feeling her, but he didn't know if they were gon' take their relationship to the next level because she was married. Listening to him talk about his feelings for another woman told me there will never be an us again, so I would have to live with his decision. Since Taylor and I needed to keep things casual, we needed to have a talk, but this time, I hoped it all went well.

Chapter Fifteen:
Chaz

Seeing Devyn lying in her own blood, scared the shit out of me. I was so glad she was ok and able to leave the hospital today. After she got cleared to go home, we left out the hospital and headed to my parents' house to pick Cassie up. Ten minutes went by and we were pulling up in my parent's driveway. My mama cooked breakfast, so she told me and Devyn to come inside. Once I helped Devyn out the car and up the steps, my pops was opening the door.

"Pops, how are you feeling?" Devyn asked.

"I'm good, sweetheart, but I should be asking you how you're feeling."

"Oh, I'm okay, just in a little pain, that's all."

"I'm glad to know you're doing good, Devyn. I know I never really say much, but you need to stay out of bad situations. You have my grand princess to live for and if you not gon' get right for no one else, make sure you do it for her."

My pops spoke some truth to Devyn before we headed inside the house. My parents didn't dislike Devyn or down talk her, but they hoped one day she would change her life for the better. They knew all about her family and how she grew up, so a lot of the shit she did was expected. They just always instilled in me, I needed to be the best dad I could be.

Once we made it inside the house, I walked Devyn into the living room, so she could sit on the couch.

"I'll be right back with something to drink, so you can take your pain pills."

"Okay, Chaz, thank you," Devyn replied, and I headed to the kitchen.

Mama was setting the table, so I walked over to her and placed a kiss on her cheek.

"Hey, Mama, what you got going on in here. It smells good."

"Good morning, baby, I got everything going on; pancakes, bacon, sausage, fish, grits, and cheese eggs. Where's Devyn, I thought she was coming with you?"

"She's in the living room. I didn't know you were ready for us to eat yet. I came in here to get her a bottled water, so she can take her pain pills."

"Oh, okay, how's she doing?"

"I think she's doing well, considering what she just went through. Where's Cassie, she wants to see her."

As soon as I said that, my pop came walking in the kitchen with Cassie on his back.

"DADDY!" Cassie screamed.

"Princess, you just blew my eardrums," Pop said while laughing.

I swear I loved my family and how they interacted with Cassie.

"Hey, baby, come here, so we can go see your mommy."

"Yayyyyyyy, mommy!" Cassie yelled as I took her from my pops.

Once I had her in my arms, I headed to the living room, so she could see her mom. When we made it to the living room, Devyn was asleep just that fast. Cassie nearly jumped out of my arms when she saw her.

"Be careful, Princess, before you fall."

She walked over to Devyn, leaned over, and kissed her on her cheek. Devyn woke up from her sleep.

"Hey, cupcake, what are you doing?"

"Hey, Mommy, I kiss your cheek."

"Thank you for the kiss, baby."

Devyn said as she tried to sit up. I could see the pain in her face, which reminded me I'd left her water in the kitchen.

"I forgot your water in the kitchen, my fault, ma. Mama said come on in the there anyway, so we can eat while the food is hot."

I held my arm out, so Devyn could grab it, and I could help pull her up. She walked and moved on her own, but really slow, due to all the pain she was in.

"Ouch! Shit!"

"Oooooooh, Daddy, Mommy said a bad word."

I gave Devyn the side eye before I smiled. I knew she didn't mean to curse, but I had to look serious for Cassie.

"I'm sorry, cupcake. Mommy didn't mean to say a bad word."

After I made sure Devyn was alright, we headed to the kitchen where Mama and Pop were waiting for us.

"It's about time y'all got in here, I'm hungry as hell," Pop fussed.

"Rome, watch your mouth, you see Cassie in here," Mama D fussed back.

I knew it was coming because those two did nothing but fuss at each other, but the love they had for one another was so real.

"D, don't start, nobody, trying to hear you yapping today. "

"Shut up and eat, Rome," Mama D yelled.

Pop did exactly what she said and started eating.

"Y'all two stay arguing with each other," I said while chuckling.

"Chaz, wait until you get married and grow old with someone, you'll be doing the same thing. Hey, Devyn, how are you feeling today, baby?" Mama inquired.

"I'm okay, Mama D, and thanks for having me over for breakfast."

"No thanks needed, baby. You're my grand baby's mom, so that makes you family."

We all sat, ate, talked, and spent the morning at my parents' house. I ended up taking Devyn home, then headed to my crib.

****

Pulling into my driveway, I noticed Taylor was sitting outside my house. I didn't know why she was even there. The way she talked to me was unacceptable and I wasn't really beat for her attitude today. I hopped out of my car after hitting the lock button, then headed for my door, making sure to walk right past Taylor.

"I know you see me sitting here, Chaz."

"What do you want, Tay? If you came here to argue, then I'm letting you know now I'm not in the mood."

"I'm not here to argue. I just think we need to talk."

"We can talk, but as soon as you start getting loud, I'm telling you now, you can leave. Now, if you think you can talk to me like you have good sense, then come on," I said while heading in my house with Taylor following closely behind.

"Are you okay? You seem like something's bothering you."

"I'm good, Tay, just had a long night. Now, what's up?"

"I wanted to tell you that I understand what you meant about us fighting in front of your house. I get that you think it should've been handled differently, but I was always taught that if someone hit me, to hit them back. I couldn't just let your baby mama hit me and I didn't react to it. That would've just been crazy."

"I thought about it after you left and I was gon' apologize to you for snapping on you like that. The only thing that came to mind was what if Cassie were here. I understand where you're coming from, but if Cassie were here, would you have walked away?"

"To be honest with you, I probably would've still hit her ass, but know that it was a natural reflex."

I looked at her and laughed; she was truly something else.

"Come here, crazy." I held my arms out, so I could pull her in for a hug.

"I'm sorry, Chaz, for snapping on you last night. I was still in my feelings about the situation with Devyn."

"I knew you were, but the next time I tell your little ass I'm handling something, listen to me. The reason I couldn't talk is because I was at the hospital with Devyn all night. When I took Cassie over to see her, she was unconscious."

I went ahead and told Taylor where I was in case she found out about it from someone else. I didn't want her to think I was trying to hide anything from her.

"Oh, my, God, Chaz, is she alright?"

"Yeah, she's cool. I just dropped her off at home."

"No wonder you look exhausted. How about we go upstairs and take a nap? My night was long as well."

"So, we cool? No more attitudes, right?"

"I'm cool, Chaz. You know I can't stay mad at you long," Taylor replied before we headed up the stairs and climbed into the bed.

It wasn't long until we both drifted off to sleep. That nap we were about to take was well needed.

Chapter Sixteen:

Keon

Raven thought she was sneaky, but I was gone catch her sucka ass dude somewhere. I couldn't believe that bitch got a new nigga already. That showed me she didn't give a fuck about me anyway.

"Yo, what's good, y'all?" I inquired while walking up on the block where I often did my business.

"What's good, Keon?" My boy, Jake, asked while dapping me up.

"Nothing much, I just got into it with some dude my girl fuckin' with."

"Say word? So, what happened? Do that nigga need to be handled?"

"Hell yeah, as soon as I see his ass. But, first, I wanna rob that place where he works."

"What place he work at? I'm always down for some extra easy cash."

"He works at a spot called Chaz' place."

See, that night after I left the jail, I did my research on that nigga and found out he worked for Chaz. Me and Chaz knew each other from back in the day, but I didn't know he worked with that bitch ass nigga, Levi. While I didn't want to have a problem with Chaz, something told me that if I went after Levi, Chaz would put a target on my back.

"Oh, that's a big hit, my nigga. We gon' need a couple of people. I heard that place makes mad cash, so you know I'm down; just keep me posted."

"I'm gone do a little more research and find out when their busiest nights are, then I'ma get a crew together, so we can do this shit right."

"That nigga must've pissed you off bad as hell."

"Yeah, he came at me, now I'ma fuck with him."

"Well, what does the owner got to do with this?"

"Nothing really, but I know they run together. So, if I come for the friend, I'ma have to handle them both," I barked not giving a damn if anybody had a problem with what I was trying to do.

"Oh, okay, well get at me when you ready. You know I'm down."

After I was done bussing it up with those niggas, I headed across the street to my mama's house. There was something fucking with me that kept me from getting comfortable. Not being with Raven or Devyn had me all fucked up. If only Devyn would've made up her fuckin' mind a long time ago, I wouldn't have even messed with Raven. I opened my mama's door and went straight up the steps.

"Don't be just walking in my fuckin' house without speaking to me, you fuckin' asshole," my mama screamed, so I knew her ass was drunk, as usual.

All she did was drink all day and it's been that way since I was younger. My dad would cheat on her and leave us for a few days, so she would turn to the bottle.

"Mama, gon' ahead with all that shit. I said hello to you before I left."

"I don't care when you said it, this is my muthafuckin' house and if you don't like to speak to me when you come in, then you can fuckin' leave."

"Don't even worry about it, Mama. I'ma be gone real soon."

After I said what I said, I went up to my room and made sure to shut the door and lock it behind me. Lying down on my bed, thoughts of Devyn came into my head. I kind of still was in my feelings about the shit that went down between us, and I've been thinking about my seed. I pulled out my phone and dialed her number to see what she was doing.

"Hello," Devyn answered sounding all groggily.

"Hey, ma, what's going on? Why you sound like that?"

"I just came from the hospital, Keon, and I'm in a lot of pain. What's up? What made you call me?"

"What happened; why were you in the hospital?"

"I lost the baby, Keon," Devyn said.

I could hear the sadness in her voice and that fucked me up bad.

"Damn, ma, I'm sorry to hear that."

"You're not sorry, Keon. Remember you didn't even want the baby," was the last thing Devyn said before she hung up in my ear.

She was right, I was glad that she'd lost the baby. Not saying I wouldn't have been there for my seed, but having a baby around would make it that much harder for me to get Raven back, and I wasn't trying to lose her for good.

Deciding to try to talk Raven again, I headed to the home we once shared. When I pulled into the driveway, I was surprised to see her car replaced with a car I'd never seen before. I figured Raven must've traded in the car I gave her, and went and got a new one. That was the only thing I could've thought had happened at that time.

Stepping out of my car, I headed up the driveway towards the front door. I attempted to use the key I had to walk in and surprise her. But, to my surprise, the damn door wouldn't open. That bitch had changed the locks on me. I couldn't believe she'd go that damn far, knowing we always broke up and got back together.

Frustrated with the entire situation, I beat on the door with my fist. When I didn't get a response, I grew even more frustrated, I turned around and kicked the door with the bottom of my shoe. After kicking it about five times, someone snatched the door open. Not seeing the door had been opened, I kicked again and ended up falling inside the house. Lying on my back, I looked up and noticed that the same nigga that was at the jail, was standing over me. I almost lost my mind until I realized he had a gun aimed at my head.

"Why the fuck you kicking on my girl's door?" He inquired, further upsetting me.

"I got this, Levi."

Raven came from out of nowhere and stood next to that nigga aiming her gun at me as if they were on some Bonnie and Clyde type shit.

I struggled to get up, but managed to rise to my feet. I found myself engaged in a stare off with that nigga, Levi. Raven stepped between us as if she needed to protect him, never taking her gun down. I knew Raven was crazy, but I didn't know she was crazy enough to shoot me over another nigga. Had I really lost my girl for good?

Chapter Seventeen:
Raven

Keon had a lot of nerve showing up at my house like he still lived here. We saw his dumbass when he pulled up and when he called himself using his key to get in. You damn right, I changed my locks on him. I wasn't a fool. I'd seen enough movies to know when a woman put a man out because he was in the wrong, that nigga would do everything in his power to try not to lose his good thing.

"Why are you here, Keon?"

"I wanted to talk to you. We can't seriously be over without you giving me the chance to make things right."

I allowed him time to finish his statement before I lit into his ass.

"Okay, you want to talk, right?"

He nodded his head.

"Then let's talk. Let's talk about how I was too damn good to you, cooking, cleaning, and washing your funky drawers while you ran the streets all times of the day and night. You barely showed me any attention and brought home laundromat money. But, I stayed. I stayed because I loved you. I was willing to be the breadwinner and have my man's back until he either got tired of not bringing home shit and do better or decided that he wanted more for himself and bossed up in the streets. Even that wasn't good enough for your ass, right?"

"But Ra-." I threw my hands up to stop him.

"Don't you say shit. You had months to tell me you weren't happy, but you never opened your damn mouth, so don't open that bitch now. I settled for that lil dick you worked with cuz' your head game was Ford tough. I settled for the many lies and excuses you gave me while you went and laid up with the next bitch. And do I need to mention that you couldn't even protect yourself? You got that bitch pregnant!" Keon looked at me in shock.

Levi spoke with Chaz earlier today and he told us about Devyn and the baby. It hurt me to the core when I found out that Keon had gotten another bitch pregnant, but I had to keep it cool for the sake of my relationship with Levi.

"She lost the baby." Keon's voice cracked as he told me that.

Now, I'm sure he was expecting me to show some type of concern for what he was going through; I didn't. I'm sure he thought I would feel bad that his bastard seed was no more; I wasn't. He'd better catch a different bitch on, another day if he thought he would get any form of sympathy from me. I'd send his ass a *'Sorry For Your Loss'* card somewhere down the line, and insert directions to the STD clinic cuz' that's exactly where he would end up if he didn't learn how to keep his dick to himself.

"Did you hear me, baby? There's not a baby. We can work this shit out."

He must've bumped his head sometime between when he left and came back because he was clearly delusional.

"I don't give a damn if that bitch was pregnant with a dog and it died, there is no more us. There are two things I won't ever accept and that's a liar and a cheater. You're both of them, so you've already struck out with me. Now, I'll give you time to get the rest of your shit out of here, but that won't be today. I'm going to entertain my man like I was doing before you showed up. Please find your way out my muthafuckin' door."

Keon stood before me looking defeated. There was no way I was changing my mind for him. I'd be a damn fool to give up a good man for a child. That would be like me choosing to eat frog legs over steak. That shit doesn't even compare.

Keon continued to stand before me as if he were trying to gather his thoughts. There was nothing he could say at that point, so I didn't know why he was still trying. I grew tired of waiting, so I lifted my gun and placed the barrel of it on his forehead. Keon looked me in the eyes, and never blinked or flinched. He appeared to be lost. I'd never seen the look he displayed in his eyes. It almost scared me enough to pull the trigger, but no matter how mad I was at him, I could never kill him.

"You can either leave on your own or leave in a body bag," I spoke, assertively.

Chills ran down my spine as I worried about if he would try his luck. Sweat formed on my forehead and my body began to shake. Levi must've noticed the nervousness all over me because he yanked the gun out my hand and swiftly pushed Keon's ass back out the door before he slammed and locked it behind him.

Tears ran down my cheeks as I cried. The frustration, the hurt, the betrayal, the embarrassment, and a list of other emotions floated through my body as a result of the dysfunctional relationship I had with Keon. Levi didn't deserve for me to stand before him, crying over another man, so I did my best to mask the tears.

"It's okay, Raven. I know you just ended a relationship with someone you loved for a long time. I don't blame you for crying. I'm sure I would be the same way, too."

I knew he was only saying that to make me feel better, but it wasn't working.

"Levi, somehow, I don't see your grumpy ass crying over nobody," I joked, trying to imagine his hardcore ass really crying.

"You're right, I'd probably shoot their ass and go on as if they never existed." He laughed, but somehow, I didn't think his ass was joking.

"I need to go get some boxes."

"For what?"

"I need to get all his shit packed and in the garage so I can call him to come get it. At least, if he shows up again, I can just open the garage for him to get it and not have to interact with him at all."

"Do you think he's really going to go away that easily?"

"No, but I'm willing to try everything the right way before I have to kill his ass."

I'm sure Levi thought I was joking when I said something about killing Keon. Never in a million years would the thought of killing anyone have crossed my mind. Hell, I've had my gun for years and never used it because I was really all talk when it came down to taking someone's life. But, there was no way I would allow him to cause harm to me and not react in some type of way.

Today showed me a different side of Keon. He was willing to stand before me and test my gangsta. He wanted to see if I would shoot him, instead of leaving on his own. That, in itself, let me know he was crazy and was liable to do anything. I wasn't about to put nothing past him or anyone else, so I was on high alert.

"You good, baby?" Levi asked, rubbing his hands down the side of my arms.

"Yeah, I'm good. You staying here or you riding with me?"

"You know I'm not letting you go anywhere after what just happened. Shit, we bout to be stuck together like glue around this bitch until I feel confident enough that his punk ass won't try to come after you."

Hearing Levi say that made me feel a little better. Something about him made me feel protected. That was something I hadn't felt in a long time. It helped me realize that with Keon, I was just existing. Now that he was out of my life, I was ready to move on to bigger and better things. I was ready to start living.

Chapter Eighteen:
Taylor

Baybeeee, when I say it felt good to be back in Chaz's arms, I ain't telling you no lie. That nigga had arms of steel, but they were soft at the same time. Hell, they could've felt hard as a brick and I still would've laid there. Being next to him made me feel complete. I should've been left Sincere's sucker ass.

"Why are you staring at me like that?" I watched Chaz as he slept or at least I thought he was sleep until he opened one of his eyes to ask me why I was staring at him.

"You looked so peaceful."

"You do that to me, girl," he stated, then pulled me closer to him and kissed all over my face.

Playfully punching him on the arm, I watched as he pulled it back as if I'd hurt him, and fake cried. I couldn't do anything but laugh, thinking about how often I saw him playing like that with Cassie. He was a wonderful daddy and I would love nothing more than to have a child with him, but I knew we were already moving too fast.

"What are you thinking about?"

"How I need to get up and go see my lawyer. I need to serve Sincere before he tries to serve me."

"Why, tho? You didn't do anything wrong," Chaz roared, upset that Sincere may try to get gutter with me.

"You don't know Sincere the way I do. You, I, and a bunch of other people know how wrong he was, but he'll never admit it, and will fight me tooth and nail, trying to ensure he can get any and everything I've worked so hard for."

"So, what are you going to do?" He moved me off him, so he could sit up in the bed.

"That's why I'm going to see my attorney. I need to know all of my options before I make any sudden moves."

"You not about to try that therapy shit or that separating for six months shit before you decide It's over, are you?"

"No, Chaz. Why would you even ask me that?"

"Because I need to know you're all in, Tay. I can't be opening myself up to you, then you decide you want to go back to that nigga again, and leave me all butt hurt and shit. I'm not doing that, so you can tell me what you want to do now." His words to me felt harsh.

I'm not gonna lie and say I wasn't hurt behind what Chaz said, but I could understand completely where he was coming from. I left him two times before, going back home to try with Sincere, so I knew what he meant. While it crushed me knowing that he had so much doubt in me, there was no way I could honestly blame him.

"I get it. I've done that to you twice, but I promise you there is no going back after what he did this last time."

"Well, since you said all that, I want you to do me a favor," he spoke in somewhat of a whisper.

It was almost as if he were nervous.

"Anything for you, baby," I responded and got up to straddle him.

"I want you to meet my parents."

Chaz really caught me off guard with that one. I didn't want to disappoint him by saying no and I surely didn't want him to think I wasn't interested in meeting his family, but what if we were moving too fast? I didn't want to make the same mistakes with Chaz that I did with Sincere.

"Are you sure about this?"

"What the hell do you mean, am I sure? Hell yeah, I'm sure. But, if you don't want to do it, that's perfectly fine. I'm not trying to force you to do anything you don't want to do."

He tried to push me off him, but I applied all of my body weight, so he couldn't move me.

"You're taking what I said the wrong way. I don't want to be just another chick they meet. I want to meet them, knowing we're fighting to be in this for the long haul."

"The fuck kinda nigga you take me as? The only woman they've ever met was Devyn and that's only because she's the mother of my seed. Any other bitch wasn't worthy of stepping foot in my parent's house. If I'm asking you to meet them, it's because I see something in you now that I want to see for the rest of my life."

Hearing him say that, touched my heart. I could've melted right then and there. Not wanting to mess the moment up anymore, I leaned down and placed a soft kiss on Chaz's lips. I thought he would try to protest, but he didn't. He simply slid his tongue into my mouth, allowing our tongues to wrestle. I wanted so badly to feel him inside of me, but I was too amped up about meeting his parents and wanted to do it before I got too nervous and changed my mind. Giving it another few minutes for our kiss, I finally pulled away.

"What you doing, girl? I'm bout to try to slide into something wet."

"Well, that got to wait because we have shit to do."

"Shit like what?" He curiously asked.

"We're going to meet your parents."

His eyes grew big as if he were surprised by what I said.

"Why are you looking like that?" I asked, then hopped out the bed, so I could grab my suitcases out the trunk of my car.

"I know I asked you to meet them, but I wasn't talking about today, baby."

"Well, I'm ready to do this now. Besides, they'll love me. We can even take them out to eat or something. Plus, I'm anxious to see Cassie."

"Well, alrighty then. I'll call and let them know we're coming."

"No, let's surprise them." I beamed before I jetted to the car to grab my things.

When I made it back inside, Chaz was in the shower singing a song I hadn't heard in ages.

"I'm ready... (You know I'm ready). To love you... (To love you). Forever... (Forever). Come and love me forever more."

His voice was so beautiful as he sung, *I'm Ready* by Tevin Campbell.

The sweet melody of his voice caused me to become moist between the legs. I couldn't help but to undress and hop in the shower with him. I didn't even want him inside of me as much as I wanted his dick down my throat. Just the thought of the way he tasted had my mouth watering and my pussy sloppy wet.

The moment I was in the shower with him, I dropped to my knees and slowly inched his manhood inside my mouth. Soft moans escaped his lips as he enjoyed the pleasure I gave him.

"Damn, Tay, why are you doing this to a nigga?" He chirped, causing me to roll my eyes because he was interrupting my neck exercise. Of course, I had to pull his dick out my mouth long enough to speak.

"Cuz, I'ma make sure the only bitch you ever think about giving this dick to again, is me. I don't give a damn if I gotta walk around with your dick in my mouth to tame your ass, that's what I'll do," I hungrily spoke before devouring his member once again.

Chaz circled his hips in a way that matched my sucking. Wanting to give him a run for his money, I began putting in that work on his ass. Before I sped up my pace, I pulled it out, spit on it, then stuck it back in my mouth.

"Fucckkkkkk, girl, I love that nasty shit," Chaz jovially exulted as he placed his hands on the side of my face.

He caught me off guard when he quickened his pace as he started fucking my face. At the pace he was moving, it didn't take long for him to shoot his seeds down my throat. Not once did I stop sucking as I swallowed all the protein he'd given me until I'd completely cleaned his dick off. When he finally pulled out, I stared into his eyes before I licked my lips and smirked at him.

"You taste so good, zaddy," I teased, standing to my feet, so I could clean myself up.

"Fuck you doing, it's my turn to please you."

"Naw, this ain't a tit for tat type situation. I can please my man without him having to think he has to return the favor. Now, let's get ready. I'm ready to meet my in-laws." Chaz laughed at me, but never protested my orders.

We spent the next thirty minutes handling our hygiene and getting dressed. We talked the whole time we were putting our clothes on. That was something I thoroughly enjoyed. Chaz didn't mind spending time with me and holding a conversation with me about any and everything. With Sincere, it was like pulling alligator teeth, trying to get that nigga to want to do anything that involved me. I was so glad I was done with his ass, I didn't know what to do.

It took us roughly forty-five minutes to get to Chaz's parent's house because there was an accident along the way. When we pulled into the driveway, my nerves started to get the best of me and I really thought about telling him to leave. That was until an older man came out on the porch that resembled someone else I knew, but I couldn't put my finger on it.

"If you don't want to do this, you don't have to," Chaz stated as he lifted my hand off my lap and held it.

"It's now or never." I articulated as I opened the door to step out.

"Why you didn't let me get the door for you?"

"I'm a big girl, baby. You don't have to do everything for me all the time," I assured him as I stepped out the car.

"Hey, son, you didn't tell me you were stopping by." The older man, who I assumed to be Chaz's father, came off the steps walking towards me.

"I wanted to surprise you. Where's Mama D?"

"Her crazy ass in the house banging those pots and pans as usual. Who's this pretty young thang?" He probed Chaz as he extended his fragile hand out to me.

Not one for really shaking people's hands, I pulled him in for a hug. I could tell it caught him off guard by the way his body tensed up.

"Who that young heffa out there hugged up on my man?" I heard a woman's voice yell.

I figured it was Chaz's mother, so I didn't get out of character for her calling me a heffa, the way I normally would've done.

"This is my girlfriend, Taylor. We thought it was about time y'all met her," Chaz confidently simpered.

"Oh, okay, cuz you know I don't play about my man." She laughed and walked off the porch to corral around us.

Hugging Mama D as well, we talked for a moment, then went inside the house. Mama D told me she wanted to show me pictures of Chaz when he was younger since she didn't get to show people too often. Naturally, Chaz tried to stop her from embarrassing him, but she didn't want to hear it. She shooed him away and went to get her album.

As I sat on the couch patiently waiting for Mama D to return with the pictures, I studied the living room and how homey it felt. It didn't take long for Mama D to return with a big smile on her face followed by Chaz and his father.

"Girlllll, you're about to laugh when you see these pictures. That nigga used to wear a flat top and everything." Mama D's proper talk went out the window as she happily flipped through the pictures, and told me about when they were taken.

While Mama D was flipping, I noticed there was a picture she quickly turned past. With only a glimpse of it, I damn near lost my mind when I thought I'd saw someone I recognized. Stopping her from turning any further, I turned it back to the picture she tried to skip. My mouth suddenly turned parched as I saw someone who very closely resembled Sincere.

"Who is that?" I asked, having to find out for sure.

"That's our biological son, Sincere. We haven't spoken to him in years."

When I realized that Sincere was Chaz's brother, it was as if the room started spinning. I could hear everyone asking me if I were okay and even noticed Mama D trying to fan me. Not being able to take it any longer, I hurriedly jumped to my feet and ran down their hallway toward any room I could find. Locking myself in, I slid down the door and cried. There was no way I could be with Chaz knowing he was Sincere's brother.

Chapter Nineteen:
Sincere

Taylor didn't know it, but I'd been following her since the day she left our house. To say I was pissed to see her with my adoptive brother, was an understatement. I wanted to murder their asses as I watched how lovey dovey they were with each other. I began to wonder how long their little affair had been going on.

Pulling out my phone, I recorded them as they walked out the front door of Chaz's house, holding hands as they walked toward his car. They shared a passionate kiss as he opened the door and waited for her to be safely inside before he jogged over to the driver's side and got in. I waited until they pulled out and were at least two car distances ahead of me before I whipped my car out behind them.

When Chaz pulled up to my parent's house, I could've flipped out. They walked outside, embracing her as if they'd known about her for a while. Their laughter made me sick to my stomach. Suddenly, my eye started twitching and my palms started itching. I just knew I was about to lose my cool.

I waited outside for at least twenty-five minutes before I found the nerve to do something that I should've done a long time ago. Stepping foot outside my car, I looked both ways before I marched across the road to my parent's home, which hadn't changed since I had last been there. The beautiful rose bed was still full and healthy and lined the front of the house. The wicker furniture was still covering the front porch, covered in plastic. Yeah, my mother didn't play about her shit. She knew the rain would come down and the dust would fly and she didn't want anything ruining her furniture. Although they had plenty of money to buy new furniture every so often, my mother still tried to be frugal with their money.

Raising my hand toward the door, I prepared to knock, but thought against it. Why should I give them a heads up that I was there, when they didn't think to give me a heads up to let me know my brother was fuckin' my wife? I thought about sitting outside and waiting for them to come out, then I could jump up like a jack in a box, but that might've given them a heart attack. Reaching down towards the doorknob, I slowly turned it, feeling very thankful they'd left the door unlocked.

Stepping inside, I could hear a loud commotion. My parents and Chaz were standing outside my old bedroom beating on the door. The only thing I could assume was Taylor had run in there and locked herself inside. But why though?

"What's going on here?" I finally spoke, causing everyone in there to jump.

"Sincere, is that you?" My mother asked before she made her way toward me.

Holding out my hand to stop her, my father noticed my hesitation and pulled her back to him. I didn't want her coming towards me like everything was fine because it wasn't. I left because they didn't want better for themselves. They wanted to be the same old ghetto as people they were when I grew up, not caring whether people knew who they were or not. That wasn't me. I was created to be great and that's what I set out to be. I wasn't stopping until I achieved greatness, which is what I did the moment I left home. Keeping my past a secret helped me to maintain my status as a king in Taylor's eyes.

"How long have you known?"

"Known what?" My mother stupidly asked.

"You know damn well what the hell I'm talking about," I barked, causing my mother to jump.

"They didn't know, and neither did I. We just found out which is why Taylor locked herself in the room."

"You're lying."

Chaz could've very well been telling the truth, but I wasn't accepting that as an answer.

"You're a liar. You've always been jealous of me. You started by coming in to take my parents, now you're trying to take my wife. Don't you think it's time that you got a bitch of your own."

"You mean like the bitch he had for a baby momma that you were fuckin'?" Taylor picked the wrong time to step her black ass out of the room to ask me questions.

My parents gasped as they took in everything that had been said. There was no way they didn't know what was going on. Chaz had to have told them everything. None of the shit made any sense.

"Can I hug you, son?" My mother continued to walk towards me with her arms outstretched in front of her.

"I'd rather you not, but you can say you did." That was my nice way of telling her hell no.

"What did we ever do to you, but love you, and give you all the things you needed growing up?" My father finally found the words to speak.

"You really didn't do anything to me. I knew I wanted more for myself, and I could never have that as long as I stayed around y'all. Now, I'm here to take my wife home."

"I'm not going anywhere with your dumb ass. You made your choice when you decide to lay down with those other hoes."

"I said I was sorry."

"Oh, yeah, you sorry alright. You're a sorry sack of shit, poor excuse of a nigga. God should've blessed someone else with what you have between your legs because you're undeserving of it and if I could chop it off without worrying about going to jail, I would." Taylor was snapping on me, not giving me the chance to explain or anything.

I'd quickly grown tired of Taylor's antics. My parents tried to get her to calm down, so we could all talk, but Taylor wasn't having that. She told Chaz to take her home. Chaz was so shaken up by the sight of me and finding out Taylor was my wife, he stood in a frozen state.

"Let's go, Taylor," my voice blasted through the house as I stormed toward her.

If I had to drag her ass out the door, she was coming with me. There was no way I would allow my wife to lay up with my brother another night. Did it matter that he wasn't my biological brother? It certainly didn't. Shit, I knew plenty of people that can tell you there are certain people in your life that not even blood could make them any closer. That was the situation with Chaz and I. We grew up together and even though we'd grown apart, I still looked at him as a brother.

"Sin, let's talk about this shit, man. This is a crazy situation, but I love Taylor. I can't let you just walk away with her."

"What the fuck you just say to me, nigga?" I was in awe that he had the audacity to tell me he loved my wife.

I had to give it to Chaz, he was very ballsy to be able to look me in my face and profess his love for my wife. But, y'all know there was no way I would let that shit go down like that. My heart rate sped up and my breathing became heavy. I felt like a raging bull as heat flowed through my body. My father looked at me and could sense something was about to go down, which is why I can imagine he stepped in front of Chaz.

Not caring that my father was trying to protect him or that he was old as hell, I went charging towards Chaz. Knocking my father down in the process, I leaped in the air to jump over my mother trying to get to Chaz. Not getting off the ground enough, I ended up kicking my mother in the head causing her to fall as well before I ended up face to face with Chaz. He prepared to say something, but when I sent that unexpected blow to his head, that was all it took for us to become engaged in a full blown out brawl.

Chapter Twenty:
Devyn

After resting all day yesterday, I felt so much better. Following the talk I had with Chaz's parents, I decided it was definitely time for me to change my life around for Cassie, so that meant all the old shit I used to do was over. I called and talked to my old manager at Walmart to get my job back and I also signed up for an online school. Going to school wasn't for me, but I figured doing some online courses might work.

"Mama, I hungry," Cassie informed me.

"Alright, little mama, what you want to eat?"

"French-fries."

"Okay, Mama got you, sit here and watch TV."

While I headed to the kitchen to make her some fries, I heard a knock at my door. When I opened it, Chaz walked inside, looking like he'd lost his best friend.

"What's up, baby daddy. What brings you this way? You're not supposed to pick Cassie up until tomorrow."

"I know, but I just found out some shit, and we need to talk about it." The seriousness in voice had me intrigued.

"Okay, come on in, let me make Cassie some fries, then I'll be right with you."

"Daddy!" Cassie yelled, running up to Chaz.

"Hey princess, what are you doing?"

"Watching TV, you wanna come look too?" Chaz and Cassie headed into the living room while I fixed her food.

After twenty minutes, I headed into the living room with my baby's fries and some juice. I sat Cassie at her little table, then signaled for Chaz to follow me in the kitchen.

"Stay right here and eat your food, princess. Me and mommy going right in the kitchen."

"Okay, Daddy, hurry up." I shook my head and smiled because she was such a daddy's girl.

When Chaz and I made it to the kitchen, I didn't hesitate to ask him what he needed to talk about.

"So, what's going on, Chaz?"

"Earlier today, I took Taylor to visit my parents and found out some shit you'd never believe."

"What happened?"

"Mama D was showing her pictures of when I was younger and we came across a pic of my adopted brother. She started looking all crazy like she was gon' pass out, so then she asked his name. Mama D said that's my biological son, Sincere and Taylor took off running."

"So, are you telling me that Sincere is your brother, Chaz?"

"Yes, the Sincere y'all were messing with is my brother."

"That lying bastard said he didn't have any siblings and his parents were dead. I know you told me stories about how he abandoned his family once he graduated, but for him to say his parents were dead was fucking foul."

"Now, Taylor is all fucked up and act like she can't mess with me because of this situation. I'm feeling her, Devyn, and now I don't know what to do."

My baby daddy was sitting there looking for advice about another chick. That shit was unbelievable, but I could tell the way he talked about her that he was in love.

"She did just find out some crazy shit, Chaz, you have to give her some time."

"I know the situation is crazy, but I ain't trying to lose her."

"Trust me, if she's feeling you, she'll be back. You just have to let all this boil over, Chaz. Now, what are you gone do about Sincere?"

"Oh, yeah, let me tell you how this nigga showed up and walked right in my parents' house."

Hearing him say Sincere showed up had me all ears.

"What? Are you serious? What did he do when he came in?"

"He demanded Taylor come home with him, but she wasn't beat."

"How did Pop and Mama D react to seeing him?"

"They were in shock and Mama kept trying to hug him, but he wouldn't let her."

"He's a piece of shit and I wanna beat his ass. Your parents are the sweetest people I've ever met and for him to treat them like that, he needs his ass kicked."

"Me and him got into a fight and Mama D ended up getting hit and Pop ended up falling, so you know they called the police and Sincere's ass took off before the cops came. Mama D told them what happened, then went straight to her room. I know her feelings are so hurt. I wanna kill Sincere's ass, but I know my parents would never forgive me if I did anything to him."

"Damn, that's crazy, baby daddy. I'm sorry you went through all of this today." He had a sad look on his face and couldn't no one make him happy right now, but Cassie.

"Why don't you take Cassie out to the movies or shopping?"

"This is your time with her, Devyn."

"I know it is, but I'm in a little pain, so I could use a nap until y'all get back."

"Alright, thanks for being a listening ear."

"You know I don't mind. You're always here for me, so it's only right I return the favor."

After Chaz got Cassie together, they headed out the door and I went to my favorite place in the house, which was my room, and laid down.

Chapter Twenty-One:
Chaz

After sitting down and talking to Devyn, I felt bad. Although she didn't act like she felt any type of way about me possibly being in love with Taylor, I knew Devyn still loved me and was hurt by my confession. But, I had no choice but to talk to her because there was so much shit on my chest I needed to get off and I didn't have anyone else to talk to. Levi was normally the person I went to with everything, but since he'd been so lovey dovey with Raven lately, I didn't want to bother him. Even after the conversation with Devyn, I can honestly say she gave me some good advice. I just hoped I could really hold out for Taylor to talk to me before I went looking for her.

"Daddy, I tired," Cassie informed me while sitting in the back seat looking as if she were ready to pass out.

"Okay, princess, we can go home now."

Doing what Devyn suggested, I took some time away from things surrounding negativity and spent some much-needed time with my baby, Cassie. We did a little shopping, then went to get ice cream. Since she told me she was tired, I headed straight for the car, so I could drop her back off at Devyn's. When we made it to the car, my phone began to ring as I strapped Cassie in her seat. I didn't answer it until I'd made sure she was safely fastened in.

By the time I picked the phone up to answer, it stopped ringing. I didn't care enough to see who it was, so I shrugged the call off. If they really wanted me, they'd call back or leave a voicemail and wait for me to call them back. It wasn't too long after I crank the car and pulled out of the parking lot, the phone began to ring again. I rushed to answer it before the person could hang up. I didn't even bother to check the caller id to see who it was before I answered.

"Just listen, I've been thinking about what happened today, and there's no way I can just leave you alone. You've done things to my mind, body, and soul that I've never had done to me before, and I don't want to lose that," Taylor rattled off before I even had the chance to say hello.

"I feel the same way, baby. I know it's a fucked-up situation that we're in, but I'm willing to work through this."

"Me too, but I'm afraid Sincere won't let us live happily, Chaz. He's already sent threatening messages to me about me cheating with his brother and he's going to tell his lawyer everything. What will I do if he tries to get me for adultery?" Her voice raised an octave, so I could sense she was about to panic.

"Calm down, baby, you're stressing over nothing?"

"Over nothing? Are you not listening to anything I'm saying," she screamed.

As bad as I wanted to hang up on her, I knew that wouldn't do any good for my chances of us being together.

"Trust me, I heard everything you said, but let's not forget Sincere has a daughter out there. From what my parents and I heard, the little girl should be about five years old now. So, if anyone has to face the judge for cheating, it'll be his ass."

"Wait a minute. What do you mean from what you and your parents heard?"

I explained to her what Mama D told me the day we took Pops to the doctor. I knew Taylor was frustrated. However, I reminded her that I found out at the same time she did. Neither of us knew we were referring to the same Sincere, so it wasn't like I kept anything from her.

"Let's not worry about that right now. He can't say anything to you about being with me when he's done far worse than you ever could."

"Yeah, I guess you're right. I'll meet up with my lawyer tomorrow. What are you doing anyway?"

"Well, I'm headed to drop Cassie off at Devyn's because she's tired." I heard Taylor smack her lips at the sound of Devyn's name, but I chose not to acknowledge that immature behavior. "What you doing?"

"Sitting in my car, getting ready to go to your house. I really don't want to be alone right now, so the thought of being in your arms was leading me to you."

"That's perfectly fine with me. I'll be there as soon as I drop Cassie of at Devyn's, so I'll meet you there."

"Okay handsome, see you soon."

Hearing Taylor's voice changed my mood. I was so glad she'd called. I guess what Devyn said was true about giving her space to calm down, but I didn't think it would happen this soon. I was definitely thankful that it did, though.

After twenty more minutes of driving, I pulled up at Devyn's house. Hopping out the car, I grabbed a sleeping Cassie from the backseat before I made my way up the steps to the front door. I used the key I had to enter in case she was sleeping. Opening the door, the house was extremely quiet, so I knew for sure that Devyn was sleep. Not wanting to wake her, I headed upstairs to Cassie's room. After undressing her and placing her nightgown on, I tucked her in the bed. I placed a gentle kiss on her forehead before I exited the room. I knew she had to be dog tired because she didn't move a muscle when I changed her clothes. I laughed about it as I made my way to Devyn's room just to peep in and make sure she was good.

Standing outside of Devyn's room, I could hear the TV playing. I stuck my head inside the door to let her know I'd brought Cassie back home in case she didn't hear us when we came in.

"You good, ma?"

"Yeah, I'm fine. I just woke up. How was the outing?

"It was great, as usual. You know Cassie always brings me so much joy."

"Alright, baby daddy, enjoy your night and try to remember what I told you earlier. If it's meant to be, then it'll be."

"Okay, and thanks again for the conversation earlier. I really needed that."

What? I know y'all didn't think I was going to tell her Taylor was headed to the house did y'all?

"You got my back and I got yours." She winked at me. "Now, lock the door on your way out, I'm trying to watch *Power*."

After I said my goodbyes, I headed back downstairs so I could leave, but not before checking to make sure all the windows were locked and all the lights were off. I left out the house damn near skipping towards the car. Pulling my phone out, I shot Taylor a text, letting her know I was on my way, then I slid inside my car and headed for my house.

Even though Taylor and I were back on good terms, I couldn't help but think about what we were gonna do about Sincere's ass. I knew Taylor was right about him not letting us be happy, but we couldn't stop our hearts from yearning for each other. As I pondered over how much of a fucked-up situation this was, I remembered who he was and thought about how my adoptive parents would probably disown me if I ever did anything to Sincere. I could understand why they wouldn't want me to do anything to him, but in my eyes, he didn't deserve to keep breathing the same air I breathe.

A half hour later, I pulled up to my crib and noticed Taylor's car was parked in the driveway. She was sitting there waiting for me. A smile crept upon my face as I thought about it being time for me to give her a key, so she wouldn't have to always sit in the driveway and wait for me. I parked my car next to hers and got out to go tap on her window.

"Hey, ma, come on so we can go inside," I chirped while opening her car door and helping her to get out.

Once she got out the car and stood before me, I pulled her in for a hug.

"Mmmm… Let me find out you missed me," she joked, causing me to laugh a little.

"I really did. I thought you weren't going to fuck with me no more behind some shit I had no control over. That shit had me all the way fucked up," I admitted.

"I know, and I'm sorry. It just caught me off guard when I saw that pic. The shit was crazy. It was like some real-life Jerry Springer type shit."

"I agree, that shit had me fucked up, too. Sincere slept with my baby momma, too. So, trust me when I say you aren't the only one this shit has been fuckin' with."

No longer wanting to be outside, I grabbed Taylor's hand and lead her inside the house. Instead of stopping at the living room, we headed straight up the stairs towards my master bedroom. When I saw my bed, I immediately stripped everything off, except my boxers, then fell across the bed. Taylor followed suit by taking her clothes off, then came and laid next to me.

"Can I be honest with you, Chaz?"

"Of course, you can. What's on your mind?"

"Truthfully, when I learned I was married to your brother, I felt there was no way I could really mess with you. Then, I thought, what kind of man lies about his parents being dead and not having any other family. Sure, you are his adoptive brother, but you're still his brother. I was married to a man I didn't even know." Taylor's voice was replaced with sobs, and tears fell free from her eyes.

"Come on, baby, stop crying. It'll all be over soon, then you'll have the chance to be happy."

"Then, I thought about your parents and felt bad for them having to deal with this. They're never gonna want to see me again."

"They already knew how their son was, so they'll be fine as soon as all of this has passed. Don't worry yourself about it, baby."

"Why did he lie, Chaz? What was the purpose of saying his parents were dead when they weren't?"

"Honestly, the minute Sincere graduated, and went off to college, he never looked back. Sincere disowned all of us, thinking it would make him be a better man than he was when all it did was make him turn into the monster he is now. I thought the shit was dumb and really thought that nigga would come back around, but his ass stayed away for years."

"That's the dumbest shit I've ever heard of."

"Tell me about it. But, if we could stop crying over that sucka ass nigga, then you should be able to do the same. Now come over here and give me a kiss." I poked my lips out to childishly play with her.

After spending a few minutes laughing, Taylor finally leaned in and placed a kiss on my lips. We kissed for what seemed like forever before she pulled back and laid her head on my chest. I played in her hair and wondered how things would play out. There was no way I would stop fuckin' with Taylor. Sincere had another thing coming if he really thought I would let him get her back without putting up a fight.

"I think I'm falling in love with you, Chaz," Taylor said while yawning.

"I know, I'm feeling the same way," I said while kissing her forehead.

Taylor continued to lay on my chest while I continued to play in her hair until we both dozed off.

Chapter Twenty-Two:
Taylor

Feeling something cold between my legs, I damn near jumped out of bed until I realized I was being held down. My body was trembling from the chilling sensation running through my body. Peering down between my legs, I locked eyes with Chaz while he used a popsicle to add extra flavor to my already tasty treat. Chaz winked at me before he used his mouth to open another popsicle.

"Don't do this to me, baby," I softly protested, even though I really wanted him to replace the popsicle with his dick.

"Naw, remember that bullshit you pulled in the shower?" Chaz reminded me of how I tried to suck his soul out the day that I met his parents.

"But this is torture, baby."

"Well, it's a pleasurable torture," he remarked before rubbing the popsicle over my clit.

I damn near lost my mind. The warmness radiating from my honey pot instantly made the popsicle start melting. Chaz quickly replaced the popsicle with his finger. He inserted it inside of my throbbing pussy and began to slowly slide it in and out of me while he used his tongue to run circles around my clit. I could feel my juices run down my legs as I got wetter and wetter due to his touch.

Squirming all over the bed, I tried to get away from Chaz before I exploded everywhere, but he wouldn't let me go. After spending a few minutes fighting against him and seeing he wasn't going to let me go, I went with the flow. I relaxed and allowed him to take my body to new heights.

Once I'd reached my climax, my eyes popped open, and I noticed Chaz was standing up. I waited in anticipation of him giving me head or entering me, but I got nothing. That nigga walked toward the bathroom as if he didn't know I was waiting for something more.

"Wait... What the hell you doing?" I was furious he'd stopped what he was doing, instead of letting me finish up by feeling him inside of me.

"Did you get your nut?"

"Yeah, but one ain't enough."

"Girl, this ain't no Pringles commercial. You better get on with that mess," he taunted as he headed toward the bathroom.

"This shit ain't fair," I pouted.

"Life ain't fair," he retorted as he chuckled while making his way to the bathroom like I didn't tell him I wanted to get another nut in.

Instead of telling him again what I wanted to do, I got up and walked over to my suitcase. Unzipping the small compartment in the front, I pulled out the mini bullet I'd purchased a little over a month ago. When I finally opened it, I realized I didn't have any batteries.

"Aye, bae, do you have any batteries lying around here somewhere?"

"No, why?"

"I'm tryna do something," I stated without telling him what it was I was trying to do.

I already knew if I told him I was about to finish myself off with my toy, that nigga was liable to lose his damn mind. Hell, he was probably even crazy enough to say I was cheating on his ass.

"Do what? All the remotes have fresh batteries. If one ain't working, then do it the old-fashioned way."

"What damn old-fashioned way?"

"You know how people had to actually get their asses up back in the day and actually walk to the television and use their damn fingers to turn the channel."

"Negro, please. Ain't nobody about to play with you." I meant every word of that too.

I wasn't about to play with him because I was about to play with my damn self. The mention of the remote control gave me an idea. My toy needed triple A batteries, so I checked the TV remote. It used double A so that wasn't gonna work. But, when I checked the blue-ray disc player's remote, I realized it used triple A batteries, so I quickly opened the back of it and took one of the batteries out. I slid it into my bullet and was glad when it popped on.

Making my way back to the bed, I laid down on my back and placed the bullet on my clit. I turned it up to the highest speed and laid their busting nuts back to back to back.

"Yo, what the hell you think you doing?" Chaz walked out the bathroom with a towel wrapped around his waist.

"What does it look like I'm doing? I told you I need to release some more stress, but you were tripping, so I decided to handle things myself. You can't be withholding the dick, nigga."

"Oh, so this what it's about? You think I'm supposed to dick you down every time you say something about it?"

"You damn right. You know how long I've gone without getting dick? Good dick at that? Well, you should understand there's a lot I need to get out my system."

Chaz didn't say anything. He dropped his towel and stepped over it, so he could make his way toward me. Off instinct, my clit immediately pulsated. It was as if my pussy had developed a mind of its own. The way that man looked, spoke volumes to my body. I wanted him so bad I almost wanted to jump out the bed and molest him.

Climbing in bed to join me, Chaz nestled his body between my legs. I could feel his super erect penis poking me in the thigh.

"You sure you want this?" He asked as he used his dick to play at my center.

"Yes..." My breathing sped up.

I just knew my man was about to give me the business. Chaz took the bullet out of my hand before sticking his tip inside of me. I wanted to die as he pushed himself inside. He got halfway in, then pulled back once, then moved halfway in again. After the second time he pulled back, I opened my mouth to speak, but his dick came slamming inside of me. I could've shit a ton of bricks. I've never given birth to a baby before, but I'm sure it felt like the shit I was experiencing currently. I'm sure that nigga tore something up inside of me.

"So, you want me to act ugly, huh? You want me to fuck the lining out this pussy, huh?" Chaz asked, never taking his eyes off me.

I laid there staring at him with tears in my eyes. The shit hurt, but felt good, at the same damn time. I wanted him to keep going one minute, but the next minute, I wanted to quarantine myself from his ass.

"Next time I tell you that you ain't getting no dick, take your damn punishment. Pulling that lil funky ass toy out will only piss me off. This my pussy now, so I'm the only one allowed to touch it. Not no damn cat, dog, mouse, another nigga, and damn sho not no fuckin' toys. You hear me?"

"Yes daddy, I hear you."

Hell, it wasn't like there was really much else for me to say. Just that quick, Chaz had given me some act right and tamed my pussy. I bet my ass will listen to everything he says from here on out.

Chapter Twenty-Three:
Sincere

Believe it or not, I wasn't trying to cause harm to my mother or father. I loved them, I just didn't see a need to have them in my life to remind me of the way I grew up. When Taylor refused to go with me, and Chaz professed his love for her in front of me, that was bullshit, and they both knew it.

Knowing the police had been looking for me, I decided to go try to talk to my parents to see if they would be willing to drop the charges against me. Surely, they wouldn't send their only biological son to jail, right?

Parked outside in my parent's driveway, I contemplated on whether or not I wanted to face them. It had been years since I'd saw them, and really couldn't even give them a good explanation as to why I did what I did. While I thought I was doing the right thing by leaving my past behind me, it may have actually been the wrong thing.

Sitting in the car another ten minutes, I finally got the nerve to get out. I took my time walking up to the front door and said a silent prayer before knocking. As usual, my mother came to the door to see who it was. I didn't know why she'd always be the one to go to the door. It was like she was a butler or some shit. I hated that because I felt like my father always ran over her, which was probably why I was that way with Taylor.

"Sincere, baby is that you?" My mother asked, knowing damn well it was me.

I hated when people did that shit.

"Yeah, Ma, it's me." I noticed there was a bandage on her forehead.

I'm sure it's from where I mistakenly kicked her. I smirked, thinking about the incident that took place in the house.

"Who is it, D?" My father's voice boomed through the house as he walked up behind my mother.

"What the hell are you doing here? Get the hell off my porch before I call the law on your ass." My father spat, pissing me off.

"Pops, you know I ain't try to hit y'all. I was angry about what had happened. I only came here to talk. If you don't feel like dealing with me after I say what I need to say, then I'll leave and never come back."

"Son, we would never want you to leave and not come back. You're our only child. We've been lost without you," my mother spoke with such pride in her eyes.

"What I tell you about speaking for me, D? That nigga dead to me. He left us like we didn't do everything we needed to do to raise his ass the right way. Get the fuck off my porch, I won't say it again." There was so much anger in his eyes mixed with resentment and hurt.

Seeing that looks on my parents' face let me know I'd fucked up my relationship with them. While I really wasn't there to build anything with them, it still felt bad to see the hurt in their eyes.

"You're right, Pops. I fucked up. I was wrong for the way I left without looking back, but I'm here now. Can we try to make our relationship better from this day forward"

"Come on inside, Son. You hungry?" My mother quizzed.

I sure could go for a home cooked meal. I hadn't eaten shit but junk since Taylor left me.

"Naw, he not allowed to step foot inside this house. He wanted to go out there and treat us like he ain't know us, then he can continue to do so. I don't want that nigga nowhere around me." My father was serious about me not being there, so I turned to leave.

By the time I'd made it back to my car, I felt as though I wanted to cry. I hadn't felt that way in a long time. I felt broken. It was as if nothing in my life was going well for me. What the hell did I do to deserve this shit? I loved my parents, but they didn't fit into my life. Maybe I went about things the wrong way, but did I really deserve for them to turn their backs on me like I didn't exist?

"Wait up, Son," my mother called out to me.

I was happy to turn around and see her coming behind me.

"Ma, I know what I did was wrong. Trust me, I thought about it a lot, but y'all don't understand how I feel. When I got to college and started hanging around all those boys that had their shit together, I couldn't let them see that I didn't. So, I changed up everything about myself, including how I dressed, the way I talked, anything from my past, everything. I wanted to be accepted and the only way I knew how was to act like them."

"Wow, so we weren't good enough for you?" The look of disappointment on my mother's face scared me.

It was a look I knew I'd never be able to erase.

"No, Ma. I felt like I wasn't good enough for anyone. Even when I started to fit in with them, I'd distanced myself so much from y'all, I thought there was no way I'd ever be able to come back and make things right. I guess that was one thing I was right about. Look at the way pops is tripping."

"You know your pops is stubborn just like you and Chaz. He doesn't mean anything by it, he's just hurt. Just as you or anyone else would be after something like this. And let's not even discuss the fact you knocked him down and kicked me, leaving a knot on my forehead. Whether you meant to do it or not, it happened, and he can't get over that right now. Give him some time."

"What about you? Do you think you'll ever be able to forgive me?"

"Chile, let me tell you one thing bout me, I don't ever walk around bitter or upset with people because it'll only add stress to my life that I don't need, while the other person goes on about their business like ain't shit happened. I'll always love you and want you to be a part of my life, but I won't forget what happened."

"I completely understand. That's all I can ask right now. I really do want to work on building a relationship with you again." I extended my arms so she could hug me.

When my mother finally took me into her arms, I could've broken down right then and there. I missed being around her so much. I allowed my own selfish ways to keep me from seeing what was important in life which was family and love. Now, all I had to do was figure out how I would get Taylor to forgive me.

"D, get yo country ass in this house before you piss me off further. I already called Chaz and he's on his way over here to deal with this lunatic," my father barked from the porch.

"Gone ahead and leave, Son. I don't need you and Chaz out here fighting. One day, we'll all be able to sit down and work things out," my mother spoke with such confidence.

The only thing I could do was take her word for it. I reached into my pocket and pulled out my wallet. I handed my mother a check for ten-thousand-dollars and a card with my contact information on. I knew it wouldn't make up for all the lost time, but it was a start. I hurried up and dipped from in front of the house before Chaz showed up because I didn't need any of those problems while I was trying to figure out how to handle shit with my wife. Until I did get things together, my next stop was to my attorney's office. I'm sure he'd be able to put things into perspective for me regarding this overrated marriage.

Chapter Twenty-Four:
Devyn

Hearing someone knock on my front door, I tried to move as fast as I could to open it before whoever it was, woke Cassie up. Once I made it to the door, I hurried and opened it before the person knocked again. When the door opened, Keon was standing there with tears in his eyes, looking all crazy and shit. I didn't know what his problem was, but I kind of felt sorry to see him like that.

"Keon, what's wrong?"

"Devyn, can I please come in. I really need someone to talk to."

"Alright, but you have to keep it down because Cassie is sleep." I moved to the side and let him, then once he'd entered, I locked the door and following behind him to the living room.

"What's up, Ma? I see you're looking a little better than the last time I saw you. How are you feeling?"

"I'm still in a little pain from the bullet wound, but it's healing well. I'm still in my feelings about the loss of our baby, but I'm starting counseling soon. Once the doctor clears me, I'll be going back to my old job at Walmart and I've decided to do online school. So, I'm trying to get right for Cassie. What's up, though? I know you didn't come here to talk about me."

"I came here because I never apologized to you about how I reacted when you told me you were pregnant. I guess I was just in my feelings because of everything that was going on between you and me."

"Let me guess, Raven not beat for your ass anymore, so you came over here with this sob ass story. I've been in good spirits, Keon, and I don't need anyone bringing me down. I'm on some other shit and I just ain't for the bullshit anymore. Now, the situation with you and Raven, I can't even be mad about because I pushed you away for years, but when it came down to me carrying your seed and you said that shit to me, I was feeling some kind of way. I know I've hurt you in the past, but I didn't deserve that at all."

"I know, Devyn, and I'm sorry, I really am. I'm not gon' lie to you and tell you that I didn't try to get back with Raven because I did. She sent me on my way, not giving a fuck about my feelings, and I guess I deserved that for playing with hers. Me playing with her feelings had a lot to do with me still loving you. I was ready for a relationship with you, but you didn't feel the same. A lot of days and nights you put me out, I ran straight to her. I'm not justifying what I did or trying to make you think I was right. I knew I was foul, but it was the only way to help me get over how you were treating me."

Listening to him pour his heart out was crazy. No man had never talked to me like that before. I was usually the one always pouring their heart out.

"All that comes from me needing to find myself, Keon. Me not having my shit together caused me to lose my baby daddy and almost caused me to lose my life. Maybe, when I get right and start loving myself and Cassie, I can be good to love someone else. I apologize for not being what you wanted me to be, and I would love for us to start over and be friends, first. Do you think we can do that?"

"I think we can do that without a problem."

"So, what're your plans for today?"

"I was gon' go rob your baby daddy's place, but I changed my mind when I figured out Chaz was your daughter's father." I looked at him and shook my head.

"Keon, you have to change your ways, too. Do you know if you would've robbed Chaz' place, he would've killed you?"

"I wasn't thinking at the time. All I was thinking about was getting even with Raven's man. I did some research and found out info on both men. I already knew Chaz from back in the day when he was in the streets, but never knew he was your BD. It's a small fucking world."

"Wait, I didn't know you knew who Chaz was."

"Yeah, I've known Chaz for years. I guess I didn't know he was Cassie's dad because you never let me see her. I always had to be gone when she was here and all that dumb shit."

"Mama, I hungry," Cassie said while walking into the living room, rubbing the sleep out of her eyes.

"Okay, baby, go sit at your table in the kitchen, and I'll come fix you some cereal."

Cassie stared at Keon for a second then smiled and walked away.

"She's beautiful, Ma, she looks just like Chaz' ass though."

"Yeah, she always has, even from birth, but I need to tend to her really quick, are you leaving?"

"I would love to stay for a little while if you don't mind."

"No, I don't mind at all, but if Chaz shows up, please act normal."

"I'll be cool, Ma, I ain't got no beef with Chaz."

Chaz probably wasn't gon' show up, but I had to put that in the air in case he. I left Keon in the living room while I went to give Cassie her cereal and a banana. I came back in the living room and handed Keon some orange juice.

"Thank you, baby."

"You're welcome," I said as I winced in pain.

"You good, Ma?"

"I'm okay, every now and then, I get a sharp pain in my shoulder."

"Oh, okay, well, take something for the pain."

"I try not take them too much. I think they had something to do with my miscarriage, but the doctor said they didn't. I don't believe him, though. I believe if I wasn't all doped up on pain meds and knocked out sleep, I could've made it to the hospital."

As soon as those words left my mouth the tears fell. I'd been so emotional about the miscarriage, and I didn't know why because I didn't want the baby. Keon got up and pulled me in for a hug. Me being in his arms felt so damn good. With all the shit I'd been going through, a hug was definitely needed.

"Stop crying, Ma, it wasn't your fault. Even if you were awake, who's to say you would've made it to the hospital? Clean your face before little mama come in here and see you crying."

Keon was right, so I hurried and wiped my tears away, then we both sat on the couch.

"I all done, Mama," Cassie said while entering the living room.

"Okay, cupcake. Now what you wanna do?"

"Call daddy. I wanna see Nana and Pop-pop."

I pulled out my phone and dialed Chaz's number, then handed her the phone. She talked to him for about ten minutes, then she handed me the phone back.

"Daddy said get dressed, him on his way."

I looked at her little-grown butt and laughed because she was too much, but I loved her.

"Okay, well let's go get ready before daddy gets here."

"Wait, Mama, who dis?" Cassie asked while staring at Keon.

"This is mama's friend, Mr. Keon. Say hello."

"Hello, Mr. Keon. Now, come on, Mama, let's go." Cassie took off running before Keon got to say hello back.

"I'll be back, make yourself at home, turn the TV on or the music, whichever is cool for you."

"I'll be cool, Ma, just go handle your business."

I didn't know how Chaz was gon' act when he arrived and saw Keon here, but at that point, he should be cool since he has a whole relationship anyway.

Chapter Twenty-Five:
Chaz

The sound of my phone ringing woke me up from a deep slumber. I rolled over and saw Taylor still asleep, so I grabbed my phone and went to the bathroom to answer it, so I wouldn't wake her. I hurried and answered before my phone stopped ringing.

"Hey, Daddy, come get me."

"Hey, Princess, and good morning, baby. Why you want me to come get you this early."

"I wanna go Nana and Pop-Pop house, can you take me?"

I couldn't do anything but laugh at this little girl because she was something else.

"Alright, baby, get dressed and I'll be there soon to get you."

I could hear her in the background telling Devyn she had to get dressed before I got there. All I could do was laugh.

After I hung the phone up, I brushed my teeth, then turned the water on, so I could hop in for a quick shower. While I let the water run down my body thoughts of how I was ready for my life with Taylor invaded my mind. I just needed for her to get the divorce and things would be great for us. After feeling satisfied, I rinsed off and hopped out. I grabbed my towel and dried off, then wrapped it around my waist and headed to my room.

"I was wondering where you went."

"I have to pick Cassie up and take her to my parents' house, she just called and asked."

"Oh, okay, well, I'll be here when you get back. I actually have a meeting with the lawyer this afternoon, so I'll rest until then."

"Okay, baby, do you. Are you hungry? Do you want me to grab something while I'm out?"

"That would be great," Taylor assured me.

I grabbed a pair of boxers out of my drawer and slid them on, then walked over to my closet and pulled out a pair of gray sweats and a Jordan t-shirt. Once I put my clothes on, I slid my feet in my Jordan 12's and walked over to Taylor and kissed her lips.

"Why are you looking at me like that, Tay?"

"Because, baby, your ass looking good in those damn sweats." I looked at her while shaking my head.

"You so damn nasty, but I love it, though."

"Ummmmmm, I'm only nasty for my man."

"So, am I really your man?"

"Yup, mine and only mine," Taylor said, causing me to wink at her before I headed out the door.

I needed to get out of there before I ended up staying. Taylor was beautiful, smart, and the sex was amazing. She was definitely my little freak in the bedroom. I wondered why Sincere couldn't stay faithful, then again, I'm talking about a nigga that disowned his family for some bullshit that made little sense at all. I jumped in my car, then it dawned on me, I hadn't hit my parents up to let them know Cassie wanted to come over. I pulled out my phone and dialed their number. Mama D picked right up, like always. At first, I thought I had the wrong number because I heard a little kid in the background.

"Hey, Mama, Cassie wanna come over, so I'm calling to let y'all know I'm bringing her. Who's that kid I hear over there?"

"Good, bring her over, I have Sincere's little girl over here, and they around the same age, so it's perfect. Y'all two won't get along, but maybe y'all kids can."

To say I was angry was an understatement. This nigga was just on some bullshit, but now he's dropping his kid off at our parents' house. What type of shit was that?

"Mama, what is his child doing over there?"

"Chaz, I thought this was my house and I could do anything I want. Now bring my grand princess over here, so she can meet her cousin," Mama D said right before she hung up in my ear.

Yes, that shit pissed me off and I had an attitude. I started my car and pulled off. I had to adjust my attitude since I was pulling up to Devyn's house. When I got there, I noticed a car sitting out in front of her house that wasn't familiar. Once I parked my car, I hopped out and headed straight for her door. I had a key, but I was gone respect her enough to knock first. The door opened and Keon's bitch ass was standing there. I knew this was the dude she was pregnant by, but I didn't know what he was there for and to be honest, it wasn't any of my business.

"What's up Chaz, how you bro?"

"What's good, Keon, where's Devyn at?"

"She's upstairs getting your little lady ready. By the way, she's beautiful."

"Thanks, homie, now let's go have us a talk." Keon moved to the side and let me in, then we both headed toward the living room.

"What's up, Chaz? I know you're wondering why I'm here, but I assure you, I'm not here on no bullshit. Devyn and I decided to start over and do the friend thing, that's all; nothing more, nothing less."

"I understand all that, but I want better for Devyn and if you not here trying to see her doing better than you need to step. I want her to get her life on track and get right for Cassie and herself, and she doesn't need no distractions at all."

"Devyn already gave me the run down and I'm all for it. Everything she's trying to do to better her life, I'm grateful for and I'm gon' see she keeps her word, just as well as I'ma keep mine, and do better with my life, too. We grown over here, Chaz, and Devyn's a big girl. I think she got shit handled on her end."

"Alright, Keon, I hear you, but what kind of man would I've been if I didn't step to you and make sure you have good intentions, my nigga? When Devyn hurts, my seed hurts, and I ain't going for that, so just know Devyn got me on speed dial. Make sure you on your grown man shit."

"I got you, trust me, I'ma be on my shit. I ain't trying to lose Devyn. We both did some bullshit to each other and maybe starting over in the friend zone is what's best."

"That's a great idea, but if you feel like you ready to go back to your fuckboy ways, just do yourself a favor and leave."

"Daddy!" Cassie came running in the living room and jumped in my lap.

"Hey, Princess, you ready to go?" I asked Cassie while kissing her forehead, and she nodded her head yes.

"Hey, baby daddy, what's up?"

"Hey, Dev! How are you feeling, Ma?"

"I'm good today. I have a couple of doctor appointments next week and I start my online classes the end of this week, so stuff is coming along."

"That's what's up, Ma. I'm proud of you, just keep pushing and everything will work out. Let me get out of here. Mama D got Sincere's daughter over there and she's excited about her and Cassie meeting. I think she told me they were around the same age, I think."

"Oh, okay, well, that should be nice, Cassie having a playmate."

I got up and headed out the door, but not before I said something to Keon.

"See y'all later, and Keon, remember what I said, bro. If you mean well, then I don't mind you being around, but if you on some sucka shit, do me and you a favor and step."

"I'm good, Chaz, I think I got this, bro. You don't have anything to worry about."

After I said my last couple of words, I kissed Devyn on the forehead, then walked out the door. I meant every word I said to Keon and I hoped he wasn't on no bullshit. I would hate to come out of retirement and kill that muthafucka.

Cassie was in her seat and buckled in and I was now in the front seat and ready to go. Next stop was my parents' house and I hoped Sincere wasn't there because I wasn't beat. Hearing my phone going off, I picked up and saw Taylor had sent me a video of her playing in her pussy. I swear that chick was a freak. I felt my dick rising. When I got back to my crib I was gon' punish her little ass for teasing me. I shot her a text, then laid my phone down, and pulled off heading to my next destination.

Chapter Twenty-Six:
Taylor

While Chaz was gone to take his daughter to see his parents, I thought now was just as good of a time as any to finally go see my attorney to discuss my divorce. I hopped out the bed and headed straight to the shower. Turning the water on, I stopped to admire myself in the mirror. I loved the way my body was beginning to glow. Chaz was doing shit to my body that had me feeling some type of way and trust me, all those feelings were great ones.

Once I saw the water was to liking, I quickly stepped in the shower with my Dove body wash. It didn't take me long to get that tingling sensation in my skin that always made me feel clean. Getting out the shower, I wrapped a towel around my body before stepping inside of Chaz's bedroom. I could've died when I saw Sincere sitting on the foot of Chaz's bed staring at me with bloodshot red, swollen eyes.

"Aaaghhhhh…" I screamed. I wasn't expecting him to be there. "You scared the hell out of me. How'd you get in here?"

"Don't worry about how I got in here, what are you doing here, Taylor? We have a whole house you've been neglecting," he spoke in a solemn tone.

"Sincere, I'm not about to go there with you. I told you I was done, and I meant that."

"But why, Tay? We always work things out. Why are things so different now? Is it because you're with my brother?"

"Chaz has nothing to do with this. Besides, it's not like I knew he was your brother."

"But you know now, so why are you still fuckin' with him."

Sincere stood from the bed in a stance that suggested he was ready to pounce on me. "Answer me," he roared, causing me to jump. The towel once wrapped around my body had fallen to the floor.

"Sincere, you need to leave. There's nothing here for you. How'd you get in anyway?"

"It's none of your business how I got in here. Come on, so we can go home."

"No, I'm not going anywhere with you. I don't know how many times you want me to tell your looney tunes ass that."

Sincere's breathing began to get heavy, and his chest heaved up and down as he slowly began making his way toward me. I reached down to pick the towel up from the floor, and wrap it back around me in case I needed to make a run for it. I didn't want to get caught running through Chaz's neighborhood naked. He'd probably never forgive me for something like that, even if it weren't my fault.

"Come here, Tay." Sincere reached out for me, but I backed up, not realizing I was backing myself into a corner.

"Move, Sincere, before I call the police."

"And what you gonna call them on? I hope not this..." Sincere pulled my cell phone out of his pocket and waved it around as if he were taunting me.

"Why are you doing this? Why can't you just let me be happy with someone else since I obviously wasn't making you happy."

"Baby, you did make me happy. I was just a fool. Let me try to make this shit up to you."

"There isn't anything to make up. I love, Chaz. I'm done with you, and all the bullshit you put me through," I honestly confessed to him.

Telling Sincere I loved his brother probably wasn't the best idea at this time, but I didn't want to have to keep hiding the way I felt about Chaz.

"You really think I'ma let you and that nigga be together, and I not stop it? You're out of your fuckin' mind. If I can't have you, then no one else can."

There was no reason for me to continue to argue with Sincere. It was clear he'd made up his mind he was going to make my life a living hell, but that didn't even matter to me. Nothing he said or did was going to get me to be with him again. However, I wasn't dumb enough to not take his threats seriously. I watched enough movies on Lifetime to know when a muthafucka tell you that shit about "if I can't have you, then no one else will," then they meant it, and you had to really watch your back. Situations like that only left you with the option to kill or be killed.

"I'm asking you to leave nicely, Sincere." I grunted, loudly, disgusted with the way he wasted his time to sneak inside of someone else's house.

"Naw, lemme get a lil taste of my pussy," he articulated, before licking his lips.

The thought of him touching me made me sick to my stomach.

Sincere called himself getting close to me while I was backed into the corner. He thought I would back down as I would've in the past, and let him have his way, but that shit didn't work this time. I waited good until he was up on me, then lifted my knee, and made contact with his balls. He tumbled forward, grabbing himself between the legs before falling, and hitting the floor.

When Sincere hit the floor, my phone fell out of his hand. I scooped the phone up, then ran to the nightstand next to Chaz's bed. Reaching inside, I grabbed the gun he kept there in case someone decided to try him. With the gun in my hand, I moved around to where Sincere rolled around like a wounded dog.

"Now, I'm telling you again, get your worthless ass out of my man's house before I kill you. Nobody can say or do anything to me if I put a hot one in you because you were breaking and entering."

"You really think I'm going to allow you to kill me? Bitch, you're out of your mind. You must've let that nigga's dick go to your brain and shake up your brain cells because clearly, you not thinking straight," he barked as he stood to his feet.

"You heard what I said, now try me." With the gun trained on his head, I dialed 9-1-1.

It might have been best if I would've called Chaz, but I didn't want to ruin the time he was spending with his daughter with something I could handle myself. Plus, I was going to use this to start a paper trail with the police, so I could get a restraining order, and have something else to go against Sincere in our divorce.

"I can't believe you're choosing that nigga over me. Why?"

"Because for years, you chose all your other bitches over me." The look of defeat that suddenly appeared on Sincere's face, caught me off guard, but I'd had enough.

We stood there in complete silence until the police arrived. I was actually shocked Sincere didn't try to run away like he did when he was involved in the altercation at his parents' house. After the police had taken him to jail and got my statement, I was told I could go downtown, and file a restraining order against him. Of course, I was going to get it done, but I was headed to see my lawyer first.

It didn't take me long to get dressed, and out the house. I threw on a PINK jogging suit with white Air Max, threw my hair up in a messy ponytail, grabbed my shit, and jetted. I debated over whether or not I wanted to call Chaz, but decided that I would wait until he came home to tell him everything that had transpired.

Arriving in front of Mr. Fredrick's office, I swooped in one of the handicapped parking spaces in front of the building, grabbed my purse, and dashed inside. There was one person in the waiting area and his new receptionist had his back turned towards me as he talked on the phone. Since he couldn't see me, I walked straight past him into Mr. Fredrick's off.

What I saw when I walked in instantly caused me to laugh. The girl kneeled on the floor giving Mr. Fredrick's head, certainly wasn't his wife. When she turned to face me, I realized it was Nyla. Yeah, Sincere's baby's momma.

"What is she doing here?" she asked Mr. Fredrick who shrugged his shoulders.

"I can assure you, I'm not here to do the same thing your ass is doing. I have more than enough money to pay for all the services I need, so get your weight up before you decide to come talking to me sideways."

Nyla stared at me for a minute before standing to her feet. She wiped her mouth with the back of her hand, then pulled some lip gloss out of her purse to apply it before smacking her lips together.

"Baby, not even Vaseline can help you." I laughed causing her to storm out of the office.

"Mrs. Griffith, what are you doing here and where is my receptionist? Brian!!!" He roared making me turn around.

"You know what, don't even worry about it." I turned to make my exit.

Mr. Fredrick had been my attorney for as long as I could remember. The fact that he was dealing with someone that Sincere dealt with was more than enough for me to know I needed to seek new counsel. For all I knew, Sincere sent Nyla to suck Mr. Fredrick off, so he could have the upper hand in our divorce. That was perfectly fine with me because I was more than prepared to hire someone who would take everything Sincere had, including the clothes on his back.

Feeling overwhelmed with the events of the day, the only thing I wanted to do was grab a big bucket of ice cream and go home and climb under my covers. Since it didn't look as though I would be able to do that anytime soon, I headed down to the police station. If I didn't get anything else accomplished today, I was going to have that restraining order put into place to keep Sincere's ass as far away from me as possible.

Chapter Twenty-Seven:
Sincere

Taylor's bitch ass came down to the police station to press charges on me. That shit pissed me off because I didn't do anything bad enough to her that would make her want to throw me under the jail. There was no one I could call to get me out of jail, so I decided to stay there until the next morning for my bail hearing.

When I stepped inside the courtroom, I hated the fact I stood next to people that had committed real crimes. I felt like the common criminal and was treated as such. Man, that shit people hollered about being a black man in this world was hard, ain't nothing but the truth. Those cops didn't care what the hell you were arrested for. They looked at the color of your skin and treated you like shit because you weren't the right complexion.

The judge I had to stand before was a white man. I cringed at the idea his ass would probably throw the book at me. Taylor sat in the back of the courtroom as we waited for my name to be called. I kept staring at her, hoping she would at least look up, so we could make some type of eye contact, but her ass looked everywhere else around the courtroom, but at me.

"Griffith," a man with a black suit stood at the podium before the judge and called my name.

Ready for all this mess to be over with, I rushed up to the podium to hear my fate.

"Mr. Griffith, you are here because you broke into a home that your ex-wife was in and made threats to her." The man in the suit spoke.

"No, that's not true," I quickly objected, wanting them to hear my side of the story before they threw the book at my ass. "Your honor, Taylor is still my wife. She's cheating on me with my brother. I only went there to talk to her. She was the one who attacked me. Ask her judge, she's right there." I turned and pointed at Taylor.

"Please step to the podium, Mrs. Griffith," the judge ordered.

Taylor rolled her eyes because she had been called, but wasn't crazy enough to not comply with what the judge was asking her to do.

"How are you doing today, Mrs. Griffith?"

"I'm fine, sir. How about yourself?"

Was this bitch really standing in front of me trying to make small talk with the enemy? See, I knew the way Taylor worked. She was going to stand her ass in front of the judge, acting all sweet and shit, so he would take her side, and she can get them to throw my ass under the jail. I ain't have time for that shit and sure as hell wasn't about to let that shit go down like that.

"I'm doing mighty fine." The judge finally responded. "I'm Judge Anderson. The reason I asked you to come up here was to ask you what happened since you're here to actually give testimony. Is that correct?"

"Actually, I was here because I was trying to get a restraining order signed. They told me you would be the one to have to sign off on it, so I wanted to come here to see if you would, in fact, sign off on the order."

"Can you tell me what happened when you had your husband arrested."

"Judge, Mr. Griffith and I are separated because of his infidelity as well as him having a child outside of our marriage. Yes, I am seeing someone else and Mr. Griffith can't handle that. He thinks I'm supposed to constantly sit around and allow him to cheat on me."

"Shit, it ain't like you haven't been doing it," I raised my voice at her.

"And that's the very reason I'm not with your sorry as-." She caught herself before cussing. "I'm sorry judge. But, Sincere broke into my new man's house and was waiting to attack me when I got out of the shower. He even threatened to kill me saying that if he couldn't have me, then no one else can. Because of his actions, I'm concerned for my life and my safety, which is why I am asking for a restraining order."

"Man, this bitch is fuckin' my brother. She doesn't need a restraining order, she needs to go see Dr. Miami for a whole new pussy since she out there being a whole hoe."

"Order in the court." The judge banged his gavel down.

I was really showing my ass in there which didn't help my case at all. While the judge did agree to give me bail, I was ordered to take anger management courses, and he fined my ass for being in contempt of court or some shit he said. I really stopped listening when he said he was going to sign the restraining order for Taylor. That shit wasn't fair. How can someone keep a man from his wife and think he would be cool with that? Fuck outta here with that foolishness.

Taylor damn near did one of those Jed Clampett jumps. You remember the one where you jump up and clap the bottom of your feet together. If she would've, I probably would've kicked her ass in the back of the head in front of the judge because she would've been very deserving of the shit.

When I'd finally made bail, I was headed straight to my house to handle my hygiene. I'd planned on submerging my head under the water to get the dirt off me from the jail. I was only there for one night, but I felt filthy as hell. I had to call an Uber to pick me up since my car was still parked up the street from Chaz's house. Instead of having the driver take me straight home, I had an evil thought and had him take me to my car. If I couldn't get Chaz by taking Taylor back from him, then I was going to get his ass another way.

Once I was inside my car, I noticed Taylor's car pulling into Chaz's driveway. He walked outside in a pair of basketball shorts with no shirt or shoes to greet her. He even opened the door for her. When she stepped out of the car, they engaged in a long passionate kiss. That only made me angrier about the whole situation.

Cranking my car up, I put in the address to Chaz's bar in my GPS and sped there like a Nascar driver. I searched around my car for a lighter and some paper. I found the lighter in my glove compartment, next to an unfinished blunt. I hurried up and lit it up, so I could get my mind right for what I was about to do. Stopping at a Dollar General Store on my way to the bar, I grabbed two bottles of lighter fluid.

Parked in the building next to the club, I opened my trunk to pull out the hoodie I'd always kept in the car. Pulling it over my head, I grabbed the lighter fluid, lighter and two sheets of paper. Walking around to the back of the club, I tore one of the sheets of paper in half before dousing the first bottle of lighter fluid against the wall. As I was preparing to light the paper and throw it against the building, I heard a strong voice yell something out.

"Aye, what the fuck you doing?" Never looking to see who it was, I dropped everything and took off running back to my car.

Even when I made it back to the car, I still felt like the person could've been chasing me, so I crank the car up and sped away from the scene. I didn't know if God tried to talk to me to let me know I was about to make a stupid mistake or if someone was really out there watching me while I tried to burn Chaz's place down, but it didn't even matter. What mattered was the fact that I was able to get out of dodge and hopefully without anyone being able to recognize my face.

Chaz seemingly had one up on me again. First, it was by taking my parents. Then, it was by taking my woman. Now, it was because he'd put me in a bad head space. I wasn't thinking straight and was crazy enough to almost set his damn building on fire. I don't know who it was that stopped me, but I was glad I was able to be stopped before it was too late. Chaz wasn't worth me having to spend another night in jail.

Chapter Twenty- Eight:
Nyla

Dammit, she wasn't supposed to catch me in the act. Now, Sincere was going to be upset with me. See, Sincere and I had been kicking it a lately. He'd even taken our daughter to meet his parents, so when he told me he needed me to do him a favor, I agreed.

He told me it would pay off in the end and that him, Nia and I would be all set for life. Everything was going well until Taylor came busting in while I was handling my business. I knew her showing up had fucked our plan up. I rushed to call Sincere, so I could let him in on what happened, but he wasn't answering. Taylor stormed out the door, causing me to duck, hoping she wouldn't see me, but I didn't move fast enough. The moment she noticed me, she walked over to my car with a whole attitude, but I didn't give a damn.

"Roll down the window, you stupid bitch."

I wasn't a fighter at all, so I wasn't getting out the car, and I only let the window down, leaving enough space for me to hear what she had to say.

"What do you want, Taylor?"

"What do you and Sincere got going on? This nigga got you out here sucking dick for him? I know exactly how what y'all trying to do, but it ain't gon' work. Oh, and the only reason you can't reach him is because I had his stupid ass arrested earlier. Girl, I suggest you wake up because if you think Sincere loves you, that's a damn lie. He's always been a whole cheater and he ain't never did you right. Hiding you and his child from the world, you can't possibly think that's love."

I didn't even know what to say because everything she said was right. Why did I keep doing this dumb shit for a nigga that didn't care about me? Sincere just seemed so different lately. He was spending all his time with me and Nia and this morning, when he asked could he take her to his parents' house, I was ecstatic.

Since I finally get a chance to talk, you should know that my name is Nyla Joseph and I'm one of Sincere's many hidden secrets. I was born and raised in Camden, New Jersey, just like him. While he acted like being raised in a hood was a disgrace, I was just glad to be out of there. Sincere and I hadn't seen each other since we were younger until that night we ended up reconnecting at a strip club. I was doing what I did best which was hanging from a pole. After I finished my stage dance, Sincere came up to me and immediately started macking. Of course, my silly ass fell for everything he said, and he was pretty much up my ass ever since there.

Years of meeting up after the club and going to hotels lead to the birth of our daughter, Nia. While I was super excited to become a mother, Sincere wasn't happy at all, and that's when he disclosed to me that he was married. I know y'all wondering why I didn't leave him alone after that, but y'all know damn well once your feelings and a baby get involved, it's hard to leave.

"Hello, what's wrong? I know that mouth work because your ass was just using it less than ten minutes ago?"

"Look, Taylor, I ain't trying to argue with you. You're acting like you so high and mighty. Bitch, don't forget Sincere did shit to you for a long time, and you just now leaving. So, before you come around talking shit, look at yourself in the fucking mirror. I wasn't the only one that played the fool for Sincere."

That was the last thing I said before I so kindly rolled my window up, started my car, and pulled off. I wasn't gon' sit there too much longer, and let her talk shit when she was a dummy just like me. When I pulled off, I had no destination in mind, so I decided to go by Sincere's parent's house to pick Nia up. After about twenty minutes, I was pulling up in front of their house. This fine ass chocolate brother was standing on the porch. I got out of my car and hit the lock button, then headed for the door.

"Hey, Ma, how can I help you?"

"Chaz is that you?"

"Yeah, I'm Chaz, but who are you?"

See, Chaz had a face I would never forget. He was always the cutest around the way when we were younger.

"It's me, Nyla."

"Nappy scrappy, Nyla?"

"Yes, Nappy Scrappy, Nyla. I can't believe you still remember that," I said while cracking up.

"Shit, Ma, you look good as hell. What brings you to my parents' house."

"Wait... you and Sincere are brothers, I didn't know that?"

"Sincere's parents adopted me when my parents died in that car accident."

"Oh, okay, I see now. I never knew that. It's like everyone we grew up with just disappeared. But anyways, I'm here to pick my baby up."

"Wow, so it's true that you and Sincere have a kid together? That's crazy. I heard about it, but I had to see it with my own eyes."

"Unfortunately, yes, and the best thing I got out of this whole situation was Nia."

"Well, she's a little sweetheart and her and my Cassie gets along really good. Let me walk you in to see my parents." Chaz opened the door for me and I went in, then he came in after.

"Mama D, Nyla is here to pick Nia up," Chaz yelled.

"I'm in the kitchen, Chaz." We both headed to the kitchen where she had the girls at the table helping her make cupcakes.

"Hello, Mrs. Griffith," I kindly greeted her.

"Girl if you don't call me Mama D like everyone else, I know something. And what are you doing here to pick her up? Sincere said she was staying the night with me and Cassie."

"I'm sorry, Mama D, Sincere didn't tell me anything, but I'm fine with that. She looks like she's having a great time with her Nana and cousin."

"Alright, well you get on out of here, and I'll call you tomorrow when I'm ready for you to pick her up. Let us bond with our grandchild since we're just now meeting her." I guess Mama D told my black ass. I kissed Nia goodbye, hugged Chaz, and was out the door.

Today was just full of surprises. All I needed was a nice hot bubble bath and a glass of wine. Before I made it to my car, I heard Chaz scream my name.

"What's up, Chaz?" I turned around to see what he wanted.

"I wanted us to exchange numbers, so I could pick Nia up sometimes. Me and Sincere aren't on good terms, but I would love for my niece and daughter to grow up together." He handed me his phone and I put my number in.

I didn't care about Sincere and him not getting along, I wanted my daughter to get to know all of the family she had living; especially since I didn't have a big family. She didn't really have anyone on my side.

"Alright, here goes your phone. I'm all for her getting to know her family. I've been waiting for years for her to meet your parents, but Sincere would say no because of his wife, then I find out his wife didn't even know them."

"Yeah, my brother is full of surprises, but anyway, I'll talk to you soon. And please know Nia is fine with my parents, they always have Cassie. It keeps them busy since they both are retired."

"Okay, and thanks for reaching out about the girls having play dates. I'll definitely be in touch."

After I assured Chaz about the playdates, I pulled off, finally on my way home. That would be the first time in a long-time Nia wasn't home with me. I always had her unless I was working, so I was gone make the best of my time alone.

Chapter Twenty-Nine:
Chaz

Once I'd finished running around for the day, I headed home. I couldn't wait to see Taylor. I'd been missing her sexy ass all day. Pulling into my driveway, I saw Taylor's car parked there and immediately got excited. I parked, hopped out, and headed for my front door. Before I got to put my key in the door, Taylor opened it. She wore a lace body suit.

"Hey, handsome, where you been all day?"

"Out here doing a bunch of nothing, when I should've been home with you," I said while pulling her into my arms and kissing her passionately.

"Chaz, close the door, crazy."

"My fault, Ma. You shouldn't be coming to the door like this, distracting me."

After I let Taylor go, I stood for a second and admire her body as she walked away. I hurried and locked the door and followed right behind her. She wasn't headed upstairs so I was kind of disappointed. Once we made it to the kitchen she turned around and looked at me smiling.

"Come on, baby, sit down. I made dinner for you, and of course, I'm the desert."

I'd been doing so much running back and forth between the bar and my parents' house to check on them, it felt like I hadn't spent time with Taylor in a couple of days.

"Well, why can't we just go straight to desert?"

"No, nasty, let me feed you first. Plus, we need to talk anyway." I sat down like I was told and Taylor walked over to me and straddled me.

"How am I supposed to eat with you sitting on me like this?"

"Chill out, and let me help you with that," Taylor said while taking the fork out of my hand and putting some food on it to feed me.

"Mmmm, that taste good, baby."

"Thank you, I made sure I put my heart and soul in this meal just for you."

"So, you really trying to find your way to your man's heart I see."

"Is it working yet?"

"I think it's starting to work," I said while smiling.

"I gotta tell you what happened between me and Sincere yesterday, but you gotta promise me, you won't get mad. I think I really did a great job handling it."

I didn't like how that sounded and I didn't know if I was gon' get mad or not because I didn't even know what happened. Intently, I listened as Taylor told me everything that had gone down with Sincere.

By the time Taylor was done telling her story, I was furious. How did this nigga even get in my fucking house?

"What the fuck, Tay? Why am I just now finding out about this? You let a whole fucking day go by without telling me this shit? He could've hurt you, Ma."

"I had it covered, Chaz. Calm down and let me finish telling you the story. Once the cops came, they arrested him, then I went straight up there to press charges. I would've told you, but you were so busy yesterday, and this morning it slipped my mind."

"Taylor, next time some shit happens like that, make sure your ass calls me."

I was so pissed with Taylor because that nigga could've hurt her.

I didn't even feel like eating anymore. I tapped Taylor so she could stand up, and I could head upstairs to take my shower. I just couldn't get over her not calling me and telling me what happened. Sincere had not been himself lately, so anything could've happened. Once she was up, I headed upstairs with her following behind me.

"Come on Chaz, please don't be mad at me. I didn't want to interrupt your time with Cassie, then you had work to handle. I'm sorry, Chaz, I really am."

"Taylor, that was something important. Not only did this nigga break in my shit, but he could've fucking hurt you. I don't care how much you think you had it covered; your ass could be six feet under right now."

"Chaz, I can't believe your mad at me because I didn't tell you."

"Listen, Taylor, yes I'm mad, and I might get over it soon, but as of now, I'm not over it, so please leave me alone and let me be in my feelings."

"Alright, cool, I'll leave you alone, but I'm still sleeping right next to your evil ass, mad or not mad."

"You're good, Ma. You can sleep next to me, just don't touch me, you lost those privileges for tonight."

Taylor sucked her teeth, climbed in the bed, and covered up. After she laid in the bed, I headed to take a shower. I was still trying to figure out how the fuck Sincere got in my house. I swear I was so sick of that nigga. I decided I needed to find his ass because we needed to have a talk. He wasn't gon' never get used to me and Taylor being together and that was fine, but he wasn't gon' keep making her life a living hell.

Once their divorce was final, he gon' have to get used to seeing us together because I damn sure wasn't going any damn where. If he was connected to his family, then we all would know each other and we wouldn't be in this fucked up situation. Everything was that way all because of him. Don't get me wrong, I'm glad he fucked up because if he hadn't, I would've never met the love of my life. I hurried and got in the shower, washed, and rinsed a couple of times, then hopped out. After I dried off and wrapped the towel around my waist, I headed back in my room where Taylor was already sound asleep. I just stood and stared at her for a second, then smiled. She was so fucking beautiful and she was all mine. Why couldn't Sincere's ass just deal with it?

Chapter Thirty:
Sincere

Staring at the piece of shit restraining order I was served with, I couldn't help but become even angrier with Taylor. How the hell could she choose that piece of shit nigga over me? I don't even know what made her think I was going to stay away from her. This shitty ass paper?

After the incident at Chaz' Place, I went straight home to take some time to myself and get my mind right. Nobody would ever be able to understand how the situation with Taylor affected me. Maybe, if it weren't my brother she was getting down with, then I probably wouldn't care what she did. But, since it is him, I was dead set on doing whatever I had to do to break them up.

I pulled up at Nyla's apartment; I needed to talk to her to see how things went down with Mr. Fredrick. I took my time to get out the car and going to her front door because I had a feeling she was going to get on my damn nerves. When I finally made it to the door, I didn't have to knock. She snatched it open so fast I almost fell inside.

"What the fuck do you want?" she asked with an attitude as she strolled back inside.

"Well damn, hello to your ass, too."

"Today isn't the day for the bullshit, Sincere. I have a lot on my mind."

"A lot like what?"

"What the fuck are you asking for when you don't really care?" she snapped, but I didn't even bother checking her ass because I really didn't give a fuck about what was going on with her.

"What happened with Mr. Fredrick?"

"See what had happened was…"

"Don't start with the wondering thoughts shit. Get straight to the point."

That was honestly one of my biggest pet peeves. Like, why the fuck do people have to beat around the bush when they're trying to tell you something. Leave all that other none important shit out and get straight to what you need to tell me. She was acting like this was a fuckin' social visit when I was there on business.

"See, I'm talking and your ass not even listening to me. I can't do this anymore. You need to leave."

"What the fuck did you just say to me?" I needed her to repeat that shit because I knew damn well she wasn't trying to put me out of a place that I paid bills in.

"You heard exactly what I said. You're selfish and only want to use people for the things you want and need, but fuck their feelings, right? I took my stupid ass down there and sucked on that old wrinkled dick of Mr. Fredrick's, trying to help you out, thinking that we could possibly be a family for Nia when all this shit was said and done, but I was a damn fool for thinking that."

"Look, Ma, I know you pissed and you have every right to be, but you need to be mad at yourself, not at me."

"Why the hell should I be mad at myself? You're the one who told me to do the dumb shit."

"And if I told your mutha fuckin' ass to go jump off a bridge, are you going to go do it?" She was silent, just as

I knew she would be. "Look, Ma, I never told you we would be together. Maybe I said some shit while you were giving me that good dome or letting me fuck the lining out that pussy, but the dynamics of our relationship will never change. We'll be in each other's lives forever because of our daughter, but that's about it."

Nyla raised her hand in the air, attempting to slap me, but I quickly grabbed hold of her wrist. I wasn't about to let her or anyone else put their damn hands on me and get away with the shit.

"If you ever put your mutha fuckin' hands on me, I'll chop them bitches off. Do you understand me?" She nodded her head in response to my statement. "Good. Furthermore, you said I told you to do something, but it was your choice if you wanted to do it or not. I didn't force you into doing anything. I didn't put a knife to your throat or a rope around your head, I simply opened my mouth and told you what I wanted. You did it because you wanted to, not because I made you do it." I genuinely preached.

"You know what, fuck you, Sincere. I don't want you near me or my daughter." Nyla angrily spat. "You're too selfish to be around us. For years, you kept our daughter hidden because you wanted to appease your little wife and save her feelings, but what about me and Nyla's feelings? You said fuck us for years, so now I'm saying fuck you."

The shit she was saying was irrelevant to me. Nothing was going to change my mind about being with her. I'm sure she wanted Nia to get the chance to grow up in a household with both parents, but that shit wasn't feasible right now. Now, if Taylor decided she wanted to give our marriage another chance, we could see about her adopting Nia and being her mother, then she'll be able to be in a house with two parents who loved her. But, knowing that shit would never happen, I didn't bother to offer that as a suggestion to Nyla.

"I'm not trying to sit here and argue with you because it'll get to the point we'll both start saying shit we don't mean because we're angry, and that's not going to help our situation. I love Nia and will do more to spend time with her and allow her to be around my family since I know she enjoys that, but this shit between us is over. Issa Wrap, Ma."

Leaving Nyla alone was something I should've done a long time ago. I'm talking about after that first time, I should've deleted her number and stop going to that damn club, but something about her kept pulling me back. My intentions were to never break her heart but to have a great bitch on the side to fuck, feed, and maybe even finance me when Taylor was on her bullshit. I made it a point to let these bitches know who was number one in my life and they'd never be able to take her spot, but apparently, this bitch right here didn't listen.

Glimpsing back at Nyla one last time, I took my ass on back toward the door, so I could leave and go get Nia. I wanted to spend a little time bonding with her and needed to talk to my mother. Hopefully, I could get my father to come around and allow me to rebuild my relationship with him. At least, that was my plan until...

Pow… Pow… Pow… Several sharp pains traveled through my body and eventually, everything in my world faded to black.

Chapter Thirty-One:

Taylor

Chaz was being stubborn as a mule. He was keeping the dick from me because I didn't let him know what happened with Sincere. I thought I was doing the right thing, so you would think his ass would understand that. Of course, he had to be a dick about things and I wasn't in the business of begging nobody for anything.

Today, I woke up in an excellent mood. I'd located a potential new attorney and made an appointment to see her in an hour. While I was lying in bed, planning out my day, my phone rang. When I didn't answer on the first ring, whoever it was, kept calling back to back. Jumping up to see who it could've been, I wanted to throw the phone clear across the room when I saw that it was Sincere's ass. I knew his ass was already served with the restraining order and he was there when the judge agreed to sign off on it, so why the hell wasn't he following it?

Deciding not to answer the phone, I ran to the bathroom to empty my bladder. I'd been running to the bathroom more than usual lately but didn't know what was up. I prayed I didn't have a kidney or bladder infection because those bitches hurt. As I was finishing up using the bathroom, I suddenly felt the need to vomit, so I quickly wiped myself, then flushed the toilet, so I could kneel in front of it.

I'd barely turned around before everything I ate last night came up. I figured it was food poisoning, so I wiped my face then headed to the sink to brush my teeth. Of course, my phone continuously rang the whole time I was in there. Getting tired of him calling, I decided to go ahead and answer it before he got ballsy enough to show back up over here.

"What?" I screamed, making it a point to let him know I was irritated with the thought of him.

"Hello, is this Mrs. Griffith?" A voice I didn't recognize asked.

"Yes, why? Don't tell me that nigga got people calling me and trying to speak up for him. Look, I got shit to do, I'm not trying to be bothered with Sincere and none of that bullshit he got going on over there. Call his new bitch or his fuckin' baby's momma." I fussed.

"Ma'am, nobody had me call you. I found this number on his phone. I'm Detective Hombre. We need you to get down to the hospital right away."

"For what?"

"Ma'am, I'd rather not say on the phone. Please just get to the hospital as fast as you can."

While the man's voice seemed sincere, I didn't believe anything was wrong with Sincere. His ass probably puts somebody up to this shit. Then, I'd waste my time showing up and his punk ass will be there serenading my shit with a band and shit, thinking I'll take him back.

"Naw, I'm good," I told the so-called detective.

"It's very important that you get here as soon as you can. If you need a car to pick you up, then we'll be more than happy to send one for you."

"Yeah, you do that," I shouted before hanging the phone up. I wasn't about to play with those fools today. I meant what I said about having shit to do and I was going to do just that.

Throwing my phone down on the bed, I pulled my suitcase out of Chaz' closet to find something to wear. The more I thought about it, the more I realized that I'd grown tired of pulling that heavy ass suitcase out every time I needed something. Chaz hadn't said I could live with him and I wasn't going to force the issue. Plus, I needed to be out on my own. I went from living at home to living with a roommate, to living with Sincere. I needed to experience my own independence; at least, that's what I thought.

Stopping what I was doing, I ran over to the window to see how the weather was. That was how I was going to determine what I wanted to wear. The sun was brightly shining, there wasn't a dark cloud in the sky, so I knew it was the perfect chance for me to throw on a sundress. I damn near jogged back to my suitcase to pull out this royal blue and white, striped, hi-low maxi dress that I bought almost three weeks ago. I'd been looking for the chance to wear it and this seemed to be that chance.

My phone started ringing again. It was Chaz calling, so I picked up immediately.

"Hey baby, whatcha doin'?" I cheerfully sang through the phone.

"On my way to check on my business. What yo fine ass up to?"

"I'm on my way to meet Ms. Stewart."

"Fuck is that?" He barked.

"If you would've let me finish, you would've known who it was." I rolled my eyes as if he could see it.

"Well gone finish."

"She's the attorney that was recommended to me. I'ma go check her out to see if she can help me with this divorce. I'm so ready to be done with Sincere, that I don't know what to do." I told him.

When I was about to tell him about the phone call I received earlier, he interrupted me.

"Aight, well keep me posted on what you find out. I'm pulling up at my place."

"Okay, boo. I'll talk to you later. I lo-." Chaz hung up the phone before I could tell him that I loved him.

After checking the phone and realizing Chaz had hung up on me, I was pissed. You would've thought someone had shitted in my Cheerios because of the way I stormed through the room with an attitude. I hurried to finish getting dressed, threw my hair in a bun, grabbed my stuff, and headed for the door.

Snatching the door open, I grabbed my chest and screamed at the sight of someone standing on my porch. I wasn't expecting anyone, so there was no reason for anyone to have been there. I figured they may have had the wrong house.

"I'm sorry, ma'am. Are you Mrs. Griffith?"

"Who wants to know?" I snapped because he knew my name. Nobody in Chaz' neighborhood knew who I was, so there was no reason for this man to know my name.

"I'm Officer Sanders, you told the detective to send someone to get you." It was then that I realized that he was fully dressed in a police uniform.

"Where the hell are we going?"

"To Cooper Hospital."

"For what?" The shorter his answers got, the shorter my questions got.

"I'm sorry to tell you this ma'am, but your husband has been shot."

Not fully taking in everything he was saying, I had to ask him again what he said. When he confirmed that Sincere had indeed been shot, I told him I would meet him at the hospital. Not thinking about calling Chaz or anyone else, I jumped in my car and drove like a bat out of hell to reach the hospital.

Chapter Thirty-Two:
Chaz

Sitting in my office at the bar, I was checking out the footage from last night and Taylor came to mind, so I decided to call her. As soon as we got good into the conversation, something caught my eye on the monitor. I'd seen Sincere drop something and take off running, so I disconnected my call with Taylor without even telling her goodbye.

Zooming the picture in, I noticed that nigga had some shit in his hand that looked like he was trying to set my shit on fire. I wish I knew who the guy was that ran him off, so I could give him a nice reward. Man, I swear I was sick of that dude; something had to give. There was no way I could see Tay and live happily ever after with him still around. I mean, I love Tay with all my heart, but there was no way I'd be able to deal with Sincere and his bullshit for the rest of my life.

Leaning back in my chair, trying to figure all this shit out, my phone started ringing. Picking it up, I realized it was Mama D, so I quickly answered it.

"Hey, Mama, what's up?"

"Chaz, baby, we need to get to the hospital." I could hear in her voice that she was crying, so right then and there, my blood started to boil.

"What's going on, Mama, why are you crying?"

"Sincere's been shot and they don't know if he's going to make it." Hearing her say that hurt my heart, but then Taylor came to mind. I was praying she didn't do anything stupid.

"Mama, I'll be right there." Knowing that she had the kids, I hurried and disconnected our call and dialed Devyn's number.

"Hey, baby daddy!" Devyn picked up on the first ring.

"Hey, Ma, I need you to do me a favor and meet me at my parents' house. Are you able to drive?"

"I'll get Keon to bring me, but what's wrong? You sound like it's an emergency."

"It is, so meet me there now, and I'll explain when I get there." I hurried and jumped up from my seat and headed out the bar.

On my way out, I didn't see Levi, so I told Toya to tell him I stepped out and I would text him. I made it to my car, hopped in, and peeled off, hoping to get to my destination in one piece, without being pulled over.

I made it to my parents' house in fifteen minutes tops, and as I was pulling up, so was Keon and Devyn. Devyn looked good as hell today; better than she had in a minute. She walked over to me once I made it out of the car. She was still moving a little slow, but she looked great and seemed to be in good spirits.

"What's up, baby daddy? What happened?"

"Sincere has been shot and they don't think he's gon' make it. I need to get Mama D and Pop up to the hospital. I called you over because Cassie and Nia are in the house and I wasn't gone have time to take her to Nyla and bring Cassie to you."

"Alright, I'll just take the girls to my house, so y'all can go ahead. Just call me when you get the details."

"Thanks, Devyn, I really appreciate you."

"No thanks needed, and I ain't gone tell your punk ass to stop telling me thank you, as much as you do for me." I smiled at Devyn, then headed to the house to get the girls."

"Mama D!" I yelled once I entered the house.

"Baby, I'm in here." I walked in the living room and she was in my pop's arms crying.

"Where're the girls at, Mama? Devyn is here to take them home with her until we get back."

"They're in Cassie's room watching TV." I headed upstairs and got the girls. When I brought them back downstairs, I headed straight out the door with them. Once I had them in the car, buckled in, I assured Devyn that I would keep her posted on what was going on before I walked back in the house to talk to my parents.

"What happened, Mama?"

"Apparently, Nyla shot Sincere and then herself. They won't tell me Sincere's status because I'm not his POA, but they did tell me it's not looking good."

"Well, how did they know to call y'all?"

"The detective said he got my number out of Sincere's phone." The first thing that came to mind was does Taylor know. I pulled out my phone and dialed her number, but she didn't pick up. That wasn't like her, so I knew something was wrong.

"Come on, Ma and Pop, let's go see what's going on. What hospital is he at?"

"They say he at Coopers, baby."

We all headed out the door and got in my car. Pop was too quiet for my liking, but he didn't know what was going on with his son, so I understood. After we were all buckled in and ready to go, I pulled off and headed to the hospital.

****

We arrived at the hospital in no time, but I wasn't ready for that. Mainly because all my loved ones were going to be hurt. Nyla must've been really fed up with Sincere for her to do some bullshit like that. Poor Nia, Nyla didn't even think about what would happen to her daughter before she made such a stupid mistake, but I was gone do everything in my power to make sure she was raised right, just like Cassie. I helped Ma and Pop out the car and we headed inside. I walked over to the receptionist desk.

"Hello, we're here to see my brother, his name is Sincere Griffith."

"Hold on sir, let me check the computer." After she punched a couple things in the computer she looked back up at me.

"You can go have a seat right over there and the doctor will be over to speak to you guys in a second." We were sitting for only five minutes before a doctor came over to talk to us.

"Hello, I'm Dr. Pierce, I'm sorry to inform you that Sincere has passed. We did everything in our power to save him, but the bullet that hit his heart was the one that did it. We tried to stop the bleeding, but it didn't work. We have talked to his wife and she told us to let you guys handle all the arrangements, but since we told her what happened she's been sitting by his bed like a zombie." It was like I didn't hear him right and the room just got real quiet until I heard Ma scream. That's when I knew it was real.

"Noooooooooo! Not my baby, not my baby," Mama D screamed, bringing me out of my thoughts.

I had to run to her because she dropped to the floor. Pop was just sitting in the seat with tears streaming down his face. He didn't move or say anything. Next thing I knew, seeing my parents in so much pain caused the tears to run down my face. A couple of nurses came over to help me get Mama D off the floor. Once we got her up and sat her in the chair, so she could calm down, she started rocking back and forth while crying uncontrollably.

"Chaz, I need to see him; I have to see my baby one last time. Please take me to him." The doctor who told us what happened was still standing there watching everything, so when Mama said what she said, he told us to follow him.

"Are you coming with us, Pop?"

"No, Son, I can't see him like that, I just can't."

Before I took off to follow the doctor, I made sure to tell the nurses to keep an eye on Pop. Once we made it to the back where Sincere was, we walked in the room and

Taylor was right next to him in a daze. As soon as she saw me, she jumped up and ran straight to me.

"Chaz, why did this have to happen? He didn't deserve this," she said while crying in my arms.

I didn't say anything, I just rubbed her back to soothe her, while I watched my mama sit in the chair and hold Sincere's hand while she cried as well. That shit was devastating and to think, how I was just saying he needed to leave us alone. I wanted that, but I didn't want it that way. My family was hurting and they needed me right now, so I was gone do what I needed to do to make sure that they were all straight.

Chapter Thirty-Three:
Devyn

When my phone rang, I knew it was Chaz calling to tell me what happened. I hurried and grabbed it, then walked outside, so the kids wouldn't hear me talking.

"Hey, baby daddy. What's up? How's everything going?"

"Everything is all bad, Devyn. Nyla shot and killed Sincere, then offed herself, too. Mama D, Pop, and Taylor are up here going through it."

When I heard what he said, the tears started to fall instantly. All that ran through my head was that little girl was left with no parents. That shit hurt my heart like hell.

"Oh, my, God! Chaz, that poor little baby."

"I know, but I'ma do everything in my power to make sure she's good. I'm up here going through it myself, trying to stay strong enough to hold everybody else down, so I won't be able to get the girls tonight."

"Chaz, the girls are fine. Nia can stay here as long as you need her to. I don't go back to work for another couple of weeks, so I'll keep her here with Cassie."

"Alright, thank you. I'll text you when I get home tonight to give you an update."

When we hung up the phone, I headed back in the house after wiping my face, so the girls wouldn't see me crying. Keon knew something was wrong with me because of the distressed look on my face.

"Little ladies, can y'all sit here and watch TV while me and mama go get some ice cream out the kitchen?"

"Yayyyyyyy, ice cream!" They both screamed at the same time. I turned and headed to the kitchen with Keon following behind.

"What's wrong, baby? Don't tell me nothing because I can see it all in your face.

"Nia's mother killed Sincere, then turned around and killed herself. The first thing that came to mind for me was she'd lost both her parents, Keon. That's too fuckin' sad. Then, Mama D and Pops just got Sincere back in their lives, only to turn around and lose him again. I didn't know him that long, but this shit hurts his family bad."

"I know, baby, it's a fucked up situation and I feel bad for Nia. I'm sure Chaz and his family will make sure she's fine. You know you'll be around, too since she'll probably be with Cassie a lot. Stop crying and try to be strong for the girls. I wouldn't want them to see you cry."

Keon was right. I needed to get myself together and tend to the girls. I guess we could watch movies and play video games. After I cleaned my face, Keon helped me get the girls some ice cream before we headed back to the living room.

"Okay, little ladies, what movie do y'all wanna watch?"

I sat back and watched as Keon interacted with the girls, and I thought it was so cute. Looking at Keon play with the girls was so amazing. I didn't know what it was about him lately, but he was definitely different. The girls picked *Enchanted*, so Keon put it in, and they sat at the little table and ate their ice cream while me and him cuddled up on the couch next to each other.

****

Waking up out of my sleep, I noticed that the girls had laid on the floor and curled up under each other. While Keon and I fell asleep curled up on the couch. I hopped up to go get me a bottled water to take a pain pill. I hadn't needed them in a minute, so I guess I was in pain because of how I was lying on the couch with Keon. I grabbed my phone and noticed I had two calls from Chaz. It was late but one of the calls was ten minutes ago, so I decided to go ahead and call him back.

"Hey, baby daddy, are you okay?"

"Hey, Dev, I didn't mean to wake you."

"Nah, you good. How are you feeling?"

"I'm fucked up, Dev. Me and Sincere hadn't seen each other for years, then when we do, look at the circumstances. I'm in love with my fucking brother's wife, Dev, how does that shit look?"

"Calm down, Chaz, everything is going to be ok. You can't help who you love, boo. Right now, believe it or not, this is the time Taylor is gone need you more than anything. I know the situation is fucked up, but it is what it is, and the only thing to do now is to move forward from here. You have to remain strong for your family, Chaz. They're going to be looking for it since you've always looked out for everybody."

"I know, Devyn, and I'm trying to be strong, but what about Nia? She has no parents now."

"Now, you know Nia will be fine because your parents will see to that. And I'll be here to help as much as

I can. The girls were great today with me and Keon. We watched movies, played games, and ate ice cream."

"That's what's up. I see Keon has been around heavy lately. How is that going?"

"It's actually going well. We decided to just be friends first, but I'm starting to get attached. See, when me and Keon first started out, he wanted us to be together, but my feelings were still stuck on you. That's when he decided to go and mess with Raven. I wouldn't commit to him. So, I know the feelings are still there, we both were just fucking up."

"Wow, I never knew that. Well, I hope it works out for y'all. I'ma let you go, I need to try to get a nap in before Taylor wakes back up. She's been tossing and turning and running back and forth to the bathroom. This shit has her fucked up."

"Okay, just hit me up tomorrow, and keep me posted with anything you need me to do."

After we said our goodbyes, I hung up and went to wake Keon up, so we could take the girls upstairs.

"Keon, wake up."

"What's up, Ma, you good?"

"Yeah, I need you to help me take the girls upstairs."

He hopped up and picked Cassie up and took her up, then he came back and got Nia, and took her up, before sitting on the couch to put his shoes on.

"I'm about to be out, Ma. Are you gone be good for the rest of the night?

I knew we were just supposed to remain friends for now, but I didn't wanna sleep alone tonight. Hell, I didn't see anything wrong with him staying since there wasn't any sex involved.

"Can you stay with me tonight? I don't wanna be alone," I said just above a whisper.

"Sure, I can stay, anything for you, Ma."

"Thanks so much Keon, for being here for me lately. I appreciate that."

"No thanks needed, now let's go to bed, a nigga tired. Those little ladies wore my ass out today," Keon said, and I started laughing.

Once we made it up to my room, he stripped down to his boxers. I threw on a night shirt, and we both climbed in the bed together and cuddled until we drifted off to sleep.

Epilogue:

Taylor

Today was a day I would never forget. It was the day I would say my final goodbye to Sincere. I'd been locked up in the house we shared, bawling my eyes out, and wondering if his death was my fault. If I would've gone to the hospital when they initially called me, I'm sure I would've been able to talk to him and tell him that he couldn't leave me, yet. All of this was so surreal.

When I made it to the hospital, the police assisted me to the room Sincere was in. He was strapped to so many machines with his eyes wide open. I knew the tube being down his throat meant he was on life support, but I didn't know if he could hear me or understand anything I had to say.

"Can he hear me?" I turned to ask one of the nurses who had walked in to check his vitals.

"The machine is breathing for him, but he's not brain dead. We have him sedated to keep him comfortable, but right now it's on a low level, so he's alert. He will hear what you're saying."

Once the nurse explained things to me a little more, I felt better about talking to Sincere. I didn't know what was going to happen as a result of him being shot, but there was no way I could live with myself if I didn't tell him what I needed to get off my chest.

Grabbing his hand and looking into his eyes, I laid my head down on his chest. Not because I wanted to work things out with him, but because I wanted him to know that I still cared. After several minutes of lying there, I raised my head off his chest and peered into his eyes.

"Sin, I'm sorry this happened to you. I wouldn't wish this on my worst enemy. If you can hear and understand me, blink your eyes one time. If you can't, blink them twice." It took him a few seconds, but Sincere was able to blink his eyes once.

"Listen to me, okay. I don't know what the outcome of this will be, but I do know our relationship is over. I loved you so much, and yes, I still love you, but I'm no longer in love with you. You were my best friend, the person I told all of my deepest secrets to. You were also my biggest cheerleader, and supporter at one point, but somehow, all of that changed. I'm not blaming all of this on you, because I had a part in our relationship going downhill, too. When I started noticing the changes, I should've said something, I should've done what I could to fight for our relationship to go back to the way it once was, but I didn't. For that, I'm sorry. Can you forgive me?" It took a few seconds, but Sincere blinked his eyes once.

"The situation with Chaz was messed up. That's something I can also agree with you on. But, in my defense, I didn't know he was your brother. Had I known he was someone you were close to, I would've kept walking. I never meant to hurt you the way I did. If you make it out of here, I would love for us to be able to be friends, but that's if it's okay with you."

Some people may call me stupid for even offering that as a suggestion to him, but I didn't want to live my life hating him or anyone else. Truth be told, if Chaz and I decided to spend our lives together, Sincere was still going to be a part of my life because they share the same parents. Why should we have to be enemies when we're *supposed to be examples for the children who are involved in this situation?*

I'd said so much to Sincere during the time I was in there visiting with him, that things started to run together. The machines in his room started beeping causing the nurses to run in and see what was going on. I jumped back scared that maybe I'd said something to him that caused his blood pressure to spike or something.

"What's going on? Why are all these machines going off?" I asked concerned with everything that was happening.

"We're going to have to ask you to step out, ma'am." One of the nurses stated to me, but I didn't move.

I didn't want to leave Sincere, knowing that could be the last time that I would see him alive.

Something deep down inside told me that them telling me to leave was a sign that he was going to leave me. I would've never thought Sincere wouldn't be the person I spent the rest of my life with. I grew used to going to bed with him every night and waking up to him every morning. Damn, things in your life can change in the blink of an eye, I thought to myself as I watched them work on Sincere. He kept his eyes glued to me the whole time.

"It'll be okay, Sincere. You don't have to fight it. If you need to let go, then do it. I don't want you struggling or in pain. I love you; always have and always will. God, has you." I truthfully told him before I was pushed into the hallway.

The nurses closed the curtains to Sincere's room, so I couldn't see inside. I wanted so badly to know what was going on. I thought of how I could possibly slip inside without them knowing, but I was sure that wouldn't happen. The moment I walked in there, they would probably have my escorted out of the hospital as a whole.

The beeping sound was no longer there. It appeared as though the machines had been turned off. When I heard someone say, "Time of death, 13:24," I spazzed out. I immediately dropped down to the floor in a tantrum, crying, kicking, and screaming because I'd lost someone that was once my world.

These past few months between Sincere and I weren't the best, but I had to admit we did have some wonderful times together when we were happy. Although I wanted him out of my life, I didn't want him to die. They had to give me a shot to calm me down. Once they were able to get me to calm down, I sat by Sincere's bed in complete and utter silence. They wanted to admit me in the hospital overnight for observation to make sure I wouldn't do anything crazy or kill myself when I tried to drive home from the hospital, but I refused. All I wanted to do was be alone, that was until Chaz showed up with Mama D.

"You ready, Ma?" Chaz walked inside my bedroom and wrapped his arms around my waist, snapping me back to reality.

"No..." I honestly admitted to him.

I don't see how women do this shit and manage to stay strong. Burying your husband or anyone else that you're very close to is the hardest thing anyone will ever have to do in life. This day couldn't be over any sooner for me. I silently prayed the Lord would give me the strength to make it through this funeral without passing out.

"I'll be right there with you. Come on, the family car is waiting."

I was so thankful to have people like Chaz and Raven in my life. They were the support I needed to get through this trying time. Chaz' parents played a big part in helping me get through that as well. I was very glad his mother helped me get the arrangements together because there was no way I'd be able to manage everything on my own.

The service for Sincere lasted almost two hours with everyone wanting to go up there and say nice things about him. I couldn't say anything because I didn't want to stand in front of the church and lie like everything between us had been great and he was the perfect husband when we all knew that wasn't the truth.

After the service, we went to the cemetery to say our final goodbyes, before heading back to Chaz' parents' home for the repast. While everyone was inside fellowshipping, I sat on the porch, thinking about life in general and how things had turned out for me.

Chaz was certainly the man of my dreams. He came into my life during a time when I didn't think real love existed. Chaz and I had even talked about getting married, considering we're expecting our first child together. Marriage is certainly the next step for us.

Raven has never been happier. Levi has done so much to turn her life around from the reckless woman she used to be in the past. We don't get to hang out as much as we used to, but I don't mind because I know that she has someone that loves her and that'll go to war behind her.

Devyn started doing better for herself, which I'm glad about. She needed to learn to make herself happy in order for her to be able to make someone else happy. Devyn and Chaz's relationship has improved drastically and Devyn has stepped up with trying to be a better mother for Cassie, which makes things even better. Although it has only been a short period of time, I could see that she was changing into a new woman.

Mama D and Pops are still the same people they were when I met them, except, I can tell now they are more accepting of my relationship with Chaz, which I'm glad about. I didn't know what I would do if I learned his parents didn't like me. We all know people tend to look to their parents for confirmation whether a person will be good for them or not.

After Nyla shot Sincere, she turned the gun on herself. It was sad she allowed a man to get the best of her like that. She completely forgot about her daughter for a brief second and made the wrong decision for a man who was never worth her pain and suffering. In my mind, once she killed Sincere, she knew there was no way for her to cover up what she'd done. It was either kill herself or spend the rest of her life in prison. Well, you know what her choice was. As far as their daughter Nia goes, Mama D and Pops decided to take her in the same way they did Chaz. I was glad they decided to keep her, so she could get to know her family. Chaz and I get her a lot, so she can spend time with Cassie. Those two little girls love each other and we certainly love them.

Everything seems to be on the up and up for me. Yeah, Chaz started off as my cuddy buddy, someone I wanted to have some fun with to get back at Sincere, but I never thought I would fall in love with him. That doesn't matter because I wouldn't trade the love I have for him for all the tea in China. I'd stand on a mountain top and yell, I'm IN LOVE WITH MY CUDDY BUDDY, if it meant I could spend the rest of my life with Chaz.

The End...